The Mystery at the

BOSTON

MARATHON

by
Carole Marsh

Published by Gallopade International/Carole Marsh Books. Printed in
the United States of America.

Cover design: Vicki DeJoy; Editor: Jenny Corsey; Graphic Design: Steve
St. Laurent; Paste-up and trail art: Lynette Rowe; Photography of children:
Amanda McCutcheon.

Also available:
The Mystery at the Boston Marathon Teacher's Guide

Gallopade is proud to be a member of these educational
organizations and associations:

International Reading Association
National Association for Gifted Children
The National School Supply and Equipment Association
Association for Supervision and Curriculum Development
The National Council for the Social Studies
Museum Store Association
Association of Partners for Public Lands

NSSEA

This book is dedicated to Boston Marathoners past, present, and future!

This book is a complete work of fiction. All events are fictionalized, and although the first names of real children are used, their characterization in this book is fiction.

For additional information on Carole Marsh Mysteries, visit: www.carolemarshmysteries.com

Christina studies a Revere bowl.

20 YEARS AGO . . .

As a mother and an author, one of the fondest periods of my life was when I decided to write mystery books for children. At this time (1979) kids were pretty much glued to the TV, something parents and teachers complained about the way they do about video games today.

I decided to set each mystery in a real place—a place kids could go and visit for themselves after reading the book. And I also used real children as characters. Usually a couple of my own children served as characters, and I had no trouble recruiting kids from the book's location to also be characters.

Also, I wanted all the kids—boys and girls of all ages—to participate in solving the mystery. And, I wanted kids to learn something as they read. Something about the history of the location. And I wanted the stories to be funny.

That formula of real+scary+smart+fun served me well. The kids and I had a great time visiting each site and many of the events in the stories actually came out of our experiences there. (For example, we really did race down Boston's Freedom Trail, which was really long, exhausting, fun, and spooky at dusk in those graveyards!)

I love getting letters from teachers and parents who say they read the book with their class or child, then visited the historic site and saw all the places in the mystery for themselves. What's so great about that? What's great is that you and your children have an experience that bonds you together forever. Something you shared. Something you both cared about at the time. Something that crossed all age levels—a good story, a good scare, a good laugh!

20 years later,

Carole Marsh

Christina Yother   **Grant Yother**   **Jonathan Moss**   **Marty Barfield**

ABOUT THE CHARACTERS

Christina Yother, 9, from Peachtree City, Georgia

Grant Yother, 7, from Peachtree City, Georgia
Christina's brother

Jonathan Moss as Derian Thomas, 14, from Hopkinton, Massachusetts, where the Boston Marathon begins

Marty Barfield as C.F. Thomas, 11, Derian's brother

The many places featured in the book actually exist and are worth a visit! Perhaps you could read the book and follow the trail these kids went on during their mysterious adventure!

TITLES IN THE CAROLE MARSH MYSTERIES SERIES

#1   The Mystery of Biltmore House

#2   The Mystery at the Boston Marathon

#3   The Mystery of Blackbeard the Pirate

#4   The Mystery of the Alamo Ghost

#5   The Mystery on the California Mission Trail

#6   The Mystery of the Chicago Dinosaurs

#7   The White House Christmas Mystery

#8   The Mystery on Alaska's Iditarod Trail

#9   The Mystery at Kill Devil Hills

#10   The Mystery in New York City

#11   The Mystery at Disney World

#12   The Mystery on the Underground Railroad

#13   The Mystery in the Rocky Mountains

#14   The Mystery on the Mighty Mississippi

#15   The Mystery at the Kentucky Derby

#16   The Ghost of the Grand Canyon

Books and Teacher's Guides are available at booksellers, libraries, school supply stores, museums, and many other locations!

CONTENTS

1 What in the World is a BM, Anyway? 1

2 Hop on the Plane to Hopkinton 7

3 Bahstan Hahbah 9

4 A Lulu of a Lobster! 17

5 Heading to Hopkinton 23

6 It's Greek to Me! 31

7 Optical Illusion 41

8 Kidnapped! 45

9 Marathon Madness 51

10 Tater Peeler and Kitchen Rats! 59

11 Red Herrings 63

12 This is No Tea Party! 73

13 One If By Land, Two If By Sea 83

14 Time Is Running Out! 93

15 Not Till You See the Whites of Their Eyes! 103

16 Boston Common 107

17 Make Way for the Kids 111

18 Well, I Swan! 115

19 No Time to Waste! 121

20 The Finish Line 125

About The Author 133

Glossary 134

Scavenger Hunt 136

Excerpt from *The Mystery of Biltmore House* 138

Excerpt from *The Mystery of Blackbeard the Pirate* 143

1 WHAT IN THE WORLD IS A BM, ANYWAY?

"Boston is a long way from Georgia," Christina mused as she read the curious white note with the red lining once again. "I guess we'd have to take an airplane."

Christina Yother, 9, a fourth-grader in Peachtree City, Georgia, her brother, Grant, 7, and their Grandmother Mimi stood around the bright red mailbox. They ignored the bills, advertisements, and the little box of free detergent stuffed in the mailbox to concentrate on the invitation to visit Boston. The invitation read:

Mimi,

You and your two delightful grandchildren are invited to visit us during the big BM! Cousins

Atlanta, Georgia

Boston, Massachusetts

Derian and C.F. will enjoy showing the kids Bean Town! Let me know ASAP. Patriots' Day is coming soon, you know!

Love,
Emma

Mimi tapped the note with her bright red fingernail. "I guess Patriots' Day *is* coming soon. Today is the last day of March. She could have given us a little more notice."

Of course, Christina knew that didn't really matter to her Grandmother Mimi. She was not like most grandmothers. She wasn't really like a grandmother at all. She had bright blond hair, wore all the latest sparkly clothes, was the CEO of her own company, and took off for parts unknown at a moment's notice.

"Aunt Emma sure likes exclamation points," observed Christina. "Just like you, Mimi!"

"You bet!" said Mimi, giving her granddaughter's silky, chestnut-colored hair a tousle. "I'm the Exclamation Mark Queen!" She looked down at Grant who was fingering the corner of the invitation. He

Atlanta,
Georgia

Boston,
Massachusetts

looked very serious. "What's wrong, Grant?" asked Mimi.

Even standing on the curb, Grant was small. His blue eyes seemed the biggest part of him. He looked up at his grandmother. "Well, for one thing, Aunt Emma sure uses a lot of letters instead of words. What does ASAP stand for?"

Christina knew that one. (Of course, she always did!) "It means As Soon As Possible—right, Mimi?"

"That's right," said Mimi. "You can say A-S-A-P, or say it like a word—asap."

"Then I hate to be a sap and ask the next question," said Grant with a sigh.

"What's that?" asked Mimi. "There are no dumb questions, you know."

Grant slid off the curb, looking littler than ever. "It's not the question that bothers me . . . it's the possible answer. I mean what *is* a big BM?"

Mimi laughed. "Not what you apparently think it means! The BM is the Boston Marathon. It's the biggest deal in Boston each year. People come from all over the world to run in this race."

"Oh," Grant said with a grin. He look relieved, and so did his sister. "So it's like the Peachtree Road Race

Atlanta,
Georgia

Boston,
Massachusetts

on the 4th of July?"

"Sort of," said Mimi, folding the note and stuffing it back in its envelope. "Only the Boston Marathon is the oldest marathon in America, so it's really special. It has an incredible history!"

Christina and Grant grabbed one another and groaned. Oh, no! When Mimi said the word *history*, they knew they would be in for a big, long tale of everything about everything. But not this time. She ignored her grandkids' dramatic groaning and headed up the driveway for the house.

Christina chased her, running beneath the overhang of magnolia limbs over the azalea-lined path of pink and purple blooms. "Are we going?"

Grant chased Christina. "Wait up, you two!" he pleaded. He took a shortcut across the wide green lawn, weaving (against Mimi's rules) through the forest of pampas grass spewing fountains of white, feathery spikes. "Are we going?" he begged.

On the front porch, Mimi plopped down in the big, white Victorian rocking chair. She pulled out her cell phone from her jacket pocket. Grant and Christina piled into the rocker beside her. "Are we? Are we?!" they hissed, as Mimi dialed the number. They held

Atlanta,
Georgia

Boston,
Massachusetts

their breath until they heard her say, "Emma? We're coming to the Big BM!"

After Mimi hung up the phone, she jiggled the other rocking chair, causing the two kids to giggle. "What's wrong, Grant?" she asked. "You still don't look happy!"

Grant looked at his grandmother thoughtfully. "If we go to Boston, do we get to eat anything beside beans?"

Atlanta. Georgia

Boston. Massachusetts

2 Hop on the Plane to Hopkinton

By Saturday morning, Mimi, Papa, Christina, and Grant were speeding toward Atlanta's Hartsfield International airport, the busiest in the nation. Uncle Michael was taking them so they didn't have to leave their car there and "pay through the nose," as Papa, their grandfather, always said.

Grant always tried to picture how someone could pay a parking bill through their nose, but he just couldn't imagine it. Not even an elephant. Of course, Papa was always saying things that Grant didn't understand yet. His grandfather had lots of opinions. He had opinions on everything, even opinions.

"In my opinion," Papa suddenly said, "we should stop at the terminal here and use the curbside check-in, so we don't have to carry all these bags." Grant knew what that

Hartsfield
Airport

Logan
Airport

meant: Uncle Michael was supposed to stop the car right now, and Mimi had brought way too much stuff.

After a lot of slobbery hugs and kisses (Grant's opinion), and Papa grumbling about "paying through the nose" for airline tickets, they marched into the terminal. Mimi and Christina led the way, toward the newsstand to get magazines, peanut-butter crackers, Junior Mints, and all that essential airline survival stuff.

As Grant followed Papa through the door, Uncle Michael grabbed him. "Stick this in your pocket," he said. "It might come in handy." Grant felt a hand slide something into his back jean's pocket. Uncle Michael was always giving Grant weird, neat stuff that "might come in handy." This was a small pen flashlight.

But Grant didn't have time to try it out; Papa was disappearing in the crowd, and Grant hurried after him. "Thanks, Uncle Michael!" he called back over his shoulder. "I'm sure it will," he cried, as he raced after the others.

"All aboard for Bean Town!" Papa said in his deep voice as everyone scrambled aboard the aircraft.

Hartsfield
Airport

Logan
Airport

3  BAHSTAN HAHBAH

It was a great flight. Both Grant and Christina had window seats and got a good look when the pilot pointed out the Statue of Liberty as they flew over Manhattan Island and New York City. As the plane began its final approach to Logan International, the Boston airport, Christina began to get fidgety. "Why are we going to land on the ocean?" she asked nervously.

Papa laughed. "We're not," he assured her. "The airport runway just ends almost all the way to the bay." Just as he finished answering her, the airplane set down with a thud, and the engines whined as the plane slowed to a stop.

Soon they were in the terminal, and there was Aunt Emma and more slobbery hugging and kissing, and "Look how big they've grown," and all that other

Hartsfield
Airport

Logan
Airport

meeting and greeting stuff.

"Where are our cousins?" asked Christina shyly. She wasn't sure she was going to like spending time with her little brother and two other guys. Why couldn't she have a *girl* cousin her own age?

"They're down at the harbor (she said it HAHBAH) with your Uncle Fritz," said Aunt Emma. "But we are meeting them there for lunch."

"The harbor?" asked Grant. He loved boats and water. So did Papa. Mimi said a boat was a hole in the water that you poured money into. Nonetheless, she loved the boat they kept in Savannah. It was named *My Girl* after her. She used it for research and photography. Papa used it for napping.

"Boston Harbor," said Aunt Emma. (Actually, she said BAHSTAN HAHBAH, which made Christina and Grant giggle.) "Oh, c'mon you landlocked landlubbers! You'll see!"

As they had reached the baggage terminal, there was a flurry of arms and hands as luggage was grabbed off the creaking and groaning conveyer belt and piled onto a cart. Christina gave Grant a squinty-eyed "don't even think about it look!" when she saw him contemplating a hop on the carousel for a quick ride along with the

Hartsfield
Airport

Logan
Airport

suitcases. Grant jumped on the front of the luggage cart instead and got a ride through the automatic doors to the sidewalk outdoors.

Soon they were squashed into a taxi, speeding toward the city. It was a wild ride. There were tunnels and bridges and underpasses and overpasses and detours galore. "What's going on here?" asked Papa. He pointed to a mountain of dirt beside the highway.

"It's the Big Dig," Aunt Emma explained. "For years they've been digging up half of Boston to build another tunnel and more roads to help improve the traffic flow. So far, billions of dollars have been spent, and all we have to show for it is *this*."

She pointed to a multitude of very large holes in the ground filled with construction cranes and workers in bright yellow hardhats.

Grant was fascinated and had questions about everything he saw. Christina enjoyed watching the parks, fountains, and sparkly buildings speed by. She especially liked all the pretty early spring flowers. The sky was Boston blue, she decided, and the taxicab chrysanthemum yellow.

Suddenly Christina spied something that really caught her eye—a giant red lobster! The taxi stopped,

Logan
Airport

Legal Sea
foods

and everyone piled out in front of a big restaurant.

"This is the place!" exclaimed Aunt Emma. Mimi wrote in exclamation points, but Aunt Emma talked in them. Nothing she said ever seemed to end in a period, but always in an exclamation point!

"Legal Sea Foods! The best place to eat in Boston!" proclaimed Aunt Emma.

"You mean some places sell *illegal* seafood?" Grant asked. He was a hamburger and French fries kind of guy, himself.

Aunt Emma laughed. "No, this restaurant just says if the fish isn't fresh, it's not legal!" Mimi and Papa laughed. Christina and Grant just stared at each other. Maybe you had to be an adult to think that was funny, Christina thought to herself. Adults can be so weird sometimes.

Papa opened the giant doors, complete with golden lobster handles, and they all went inside. Grant spied a really neat fish tank filled with lots of colorful tropical fish. Mimi had an aquarium, but it was only filled with paper fish. She said she didn't have time to mess with 55 gallons of problems.

But what really got their attention was an excited passel of arms waving from a balcony above. Uncle

Logan
Airport

Legal Sea
Foods

Fritz flagged them down with both hands. "Here we are!" he cried. "Up here!"

Christina and Grant looked up to see their uncle and his two sons hanging precariously over the mezzanine railing like a bunch of monkeys.

"That's C.F.," Christina told Grant, knowing he would not remember since he was so little the last time they saw their cousins. She pointed up to a red-headed boy who was loaded with freckles. "He looks just like Aunt Emma."

"He looks like a lobster," Grant said, waving at the boy.

"He looks like an eleven-year-old acting like a two-year-old," Christina added. "And that's Derian. He's fourteen." She wanted to add that he was cute too, but she didn't think her brother would care. Since he might share her observation, she wisely kept it to herself.

Both boys waved animatedly to their younger cousins on the floor below. The restaurant was such a lively, noisy place that the boys' shenanigans did not even attract a raised eyebrow—not even when they both slid down the metal railing to greet the newcomers!

"Hi!" the boys said simultaneously, landing with a thud at the bottom of the staircase.

Legal
Sea Foods

Let's Eat
Lobstah!

"We're up here," added C.F.

"No you're not. You're down here," Grant corrected him.

"This munchkin must be Grant," Derian said, sticking out his hand. Grant was impressed. He took the large hand with his small one and shook it mightily.

Christina was not impressed. "He's *not* a munchkin. He's my little brother."

Derian laughed. "Excuse me, princess!" he said with a grin.

Christina blushed.

"I'm C.F.," said the red-head.

"What's a C.F.? Is it anything like a BM?" Grant asked. His big blue eyes always had an earnest, serious look. To his sister's perpetual dismay, he didn't mind asking any question of anyone, even an embarrassing one. "Mom always says there's no dumb question," he would assert when Christina criticized him for his habit.

"A C.F. is a Clarence Ford," C.F. said proudly. "I'm named after Clarence DeMar and Timothy Ford, two early winners of the Boston Marathon."

"Wow!" said Grant. He wasn't sure how long a marathon was yet, but he was impressed with everything about the Boston one already, since as near

Legal
Sea foods

Let's Eat
Lobstah!

as he could figure it was a B.D.–a Big Deal.

Before they could continue their conversation, Papa and Uncle Fritz hung their heads over the balcony. "Get up here, you guys!" they called together.

"I'm not a guy," Christina muttered to herself. The boys scampered up the steps with Grant dangling in the middle as they carted him upwards, his feet never touching the ground. Christina followed behind slowly. "Oh brother," she said to herself. "What a long week this is gonna be. I'd rather be back home reading a good mystery book."

Of course, what Christina didn't know is that soon she would be living in a mystery of her very own!

Legal
Sea Foods

Let's Eat
Lobstah!

4 A LULU OF A LOBSTER!

As soon as they were all seated around the table, a waiter brought everyone a menu.

"Yummy!" said Papa. "Look at all these choices! Fresh crab, shrimp, mussels, clams, fish, and of course, lobster!"

"Scrod, cod, you name it, and Boston's got the best!" Uncle Fritz assured them.

"Let's all order lobster!" suggested Aunt Emma.

"Great idea!" Mimi agreed.

Christina could tell that her two Boston cousins were all for this. Grant looked eager to tackle a "big, orange bug" as he called it. But Christina was not so sure. She had tasted lobster before and loved it, but she had never tackled a whole one of her very own. Nevertheless, they soon each had a bright red lobster on the plates before them and were busy tying plastic bibs around their necks. Everyone

Let's Eat Lobstah!

Let's Eat Lobstah!

picked up their shiny, metal shell-crackers and dug in.

"C'mon, Christina," Derian egged his cousin. "It's easy; there's not really a wrong way to eat a lobster."

"And there's not a neat way, either," added C.F., who was cracking into a big claw, spraying lobster juice all over the place.

Papa was helping Grant, but Christina could see she was on her own. Gently, she squeezed a claw and a big blob of lobster juice squirted right into her eye. Needless to say, the boys howled. Mimi handed Christina a napkin and frowned at them.

"Alright, you little Yankees!" Aunt Emma said. "Behave yourselves."

"That's right, boys," Mimi added. "Or when you come to Peachtree City, we'll make you eat grits."

"Ugggggggh," moaned C.F. "grits—yuck."

"Have you ever even *had* grits?" Christina asked. She was getting the hang of this lobster thing and enjoying the fat, white bites of meat dipped into warm, melted butter.

"Well, no," C.F. admitted.

"Georgia ice cream!" Derian said. "I love grits myself. And peaches and fried okra, and all that other southern stuff."

"I like northern stuff," Grant said, chewing mightily on

Let's Eat
Lobstah!

Let's Eat
Lobstah!

a big piece of lobster.

"Like what?" Christina asked. Grant had never even been north before, as far as she knew.

Grant looked thoughtful for a moment, then said, "Like snow!" Everyone laughed.

"Well, before we fight the Civil War Between the States again, let's eat up and head for Hopkinton," said Uncle Fritz. "The traffic will be murder tonight since it's Patriots' Day tomorrow."

"What's Patriots' Day?" asked Grant.

"It's the day they hold the Boston Marathon," Derian explained. "It's named for all those famous patriots like Paul Revere, Samuel Adams, John Hancock, and all those other guys with bad hair days."

"That was a revolutionary thing to name the day," Christina added, and the Boston boys groaned.

Uncle Fritz sighed. "Well, before we fight the Revolutionary War again, let's eat up and get on the road to Hopkinton. The traffic will be . . ."

"Murder!" they all cried with him.

Hopkinton was a town outside of Boston where Aunt Emma and Uncle Fritz lived, now that Uncle Fritz had retired from the Boston Fire Department.

Mimi pulled off her bib. She turned to Aunt Emma and

Let's Eat Lobstah!

Let's Eat Lobstah!

asked, "Why is Fritz so 'fight this' and 'fight that?'"

Aunt Emma laughed. "Oh, he's just getting his game-face on," she said. "With the big race tomorrow, he always gets competitive, especially since we have a family member in the race this year."

"Who?!" asked Mimi, Papa, Grant, and Christina in unison.

"Me!" a voice answered. A tall, pretty, young woman had come up the stairs behind them and sashayed over to their table. She shook her blond hair back and opened her arms wide.

"Priscilla!" Mimi squealed. "Why didn't you tell us?" she demanded of Aunt Emma.

Aunt Emma stood up and squeezed the young woman around her shoulders. "We wanted to surprise you," she said. "We thought it would add to the fun of the race if you didn't know until you got here."

Priscilla was the oldest daughter of Aunt Emma and Uncle Fritz. She was a schoolteacher who lived in Cambridge, and had been running ever since she was just a kid. This would be her first Boston Marathon. Christina hadn't seen her oldest cousin in years, but remembered all the fun they used to have when she babysat for them.

"You look like *you're* a runner," Priscilla said to

Legal
Sea Foods

Meet
Priscilla!

Christina.

"I like to run, but I can't imagine running a marathon—26 miles*!" Christina said.

"Neither could I," Priscilla admitted to them all. "But I kept running races in other towns. This year, my time finally qualified me for the Boston Marathon!"

"Can't anyone be in the race?" asked Grant. Christina knew he was picturing the gazillions of runners viewers saw on television. It always looked like half the world was running the Boston Marathon.

"No," said Priscilla, "you have to qualify for the race by having a good enough time in another marathon and . . ."

Uncle Fritz interrupted her. "You can tell them all this in the SUV," he insisted. "Because if we don't leave now, the traffic will be . . ."

Once again, they all finished in unison, even Priscilla—"MURDER!"

Christina thought it was curious how the word *murder* kept coming up over and over. She hoped it wasn't an unlucky omen of some kind.

*41.8 kilometers

Legal
Sea Foods

Meet
Priscilla!

5 HEADING TO HOPKINTON

On the way back to her parents' house, Priscilla never got a word in edgewise. Uncle Fritz dominated the conversation by telling everyone about the history of the Boston Marathon. It was obvious that he was very excited about the big day tomorrow and about his oldest daughter actually running in the famous race. It wasn't hard to catch his enthusiasm. Before long, Christina had butterflies in her stomach just thinking about her cousin participating in this challenging run.

"How did you learn all this stuff?" Grant asked Uncle Fritz, when he finally took a deep breath.

"Reading of course!" said Uncle Fritz. "My favorite book is *Boston Marathon: The History of the World's Premier Running Event* by Thomas Derderian. I bought it used at the Brattle Book Shop in downtown Boston, so it was a real

Legal
Sea Foods

Back
Bay

bargain." Uncle Fritz also loved to shop for old stuff. He was a big fan of the *Antiques Roadshow* program on public television. He also shopped on eBay on the Internet.

"Tell us more," begged Christina, as the SUV bumped through some of the narrow streets around Boston's harbor, which was busy with all kinds of boats and ships, including gigantic freighters with foreign-sounding names painted on their sides and festive cruise ships all a-flutter with colorful flags.

Uncle Fritz was delighted to be asked. He sat higher in the driver's seat of his baked bean-colored SUV and continued. "I guess you could say the Boston Marathon is about try, try, try again. You can't imagine how interwoven it is in many people's lives. In 'By The Roadside, 1854' the famous American poet Walt Whitman even wrote about the 'well-train'd runner'.

"Here's a map of the race course," Uncle Fritz said, thrusting a few wrinkled brochures toward the backseat. It seemed as if he was prepared for everything, though Christina didn't think he would be able to run in a marathon anytime soon.

Christina looked down at the long, skinny chart of places that a runner must pass to reach the finish line. It looked so short on the map, but she knew 26 miles was a

very long way. Why that was like walking, or rather running, back and forth to her school a dozen times! Whew! It made her tired just to think about it. Some places, she noted, such as Heartbreak Hill, reflected just how tough this race was.

"I'd have to eat a lot of pasta to run this race," teased Papa. Christina figured he was hinting that they should eat dinner later in Boston's Italian section which had lots of wonderful-smelling restaurants. Christina knew this because they were passing through the area, and her window was down. Umm. . . a buttery garlic scent tickled her nose. Papa winked at her and rubbed his tummy.

"Yep," said Uncle Fritz, "you have to carb-up for this race, for sure! And you have to have a good strategy." He looked at Priscilla as if reminding her of all the things she already knew. She just smiled secretively.

"The Boston Marathon has been run every year since 1897 on almost the exact same course," Uncle Fritz said.

"That's over a hundred years!" Grant marveled.

"Today, the race is always run on Patriots' Day and starts on the Hopkinton town common."

"That's where you live!" said Christina, excited to think they would have a ringside seat for such an historic event.

"We don't live *on* the town common," C.F. corrected.

Christina groaned. "Well, I didn't think you did."

"We *do* live on a farm just a couple of miles out of town," Derian added.

Uncle Fritz ignored them all. Now they were rumbling past the Charles River and the beautiful Beacon Hill section of town. Christina sighed as she tried to commit each gorgeous scene to memory.

"The early days of running were just as competitive and exciting as they are today, " Uncle Fritz explained. "The Boston Athletic Association chose a unicorn for its symbol, which may have come from Scotland. The Scottish brought track and field events to America in the 19th century.

"Native Americans were some of the first and best runners in the United States," Uncle Fritz continued. "Of course, early running was sort of funny. Everyone just did their own thing. They would run some, walk some, stop to rest, eat, drink, skip, or even crawl if necessary just to reach the finish line."

"You're kidding!" Christina said.

"Nope, he surely isn't," Priscilla interrupted. "Runners even had handlers who rode bikes, and cars later, alongside their runner to give them water or help in other ways. And what I think is the most amazing is that spectators were allowed to run wild on the course! It's a wonder the

Legal
Sea Foods

Back
Bay

athletes could even *finish* the race back then—without getting run over!"

"Some of them did get run over!" Derian added.

Everyone laughed, but Christina didn't think that sounded too funny. "Things must have been very different back then," she pondered aloud.

"Yes, they were," Mimi said. "Life was very different in the late 1800s than today. Most people worked from daylight to dark on farms or in factories. They didn't have time to do anything as silly and wasteful as running in a race. Only a handful of folks even participated in races like the Boston Marathon."

"But the rest liked to bet on the winner!" Papa added. "Those Yankee traders liked to bet the money they made from whaling, rum, sugar, and even slaves, on long distance races."

"Hey, those are my ancestors you're insulting!" Uncle Fritz said with a friendly roar. "But you're right, of course. Once amateur racing came along, with no wagering, things began to change. People were much more interested in measuring times and in the quality of athletic performance."

"So that put an end to the flimflam men," Papa teased.

"You're talking about my ancestors, again!" Uncle Fritz

Back Bay

Beacon Hill

warned. "Shall I toss him into the fen?" he asked C.F.

"What's a fen?" Grant asked.

"We're driving through what used to be a fen," C.F. said, slinging his arm out of the window. But all Grant could see was the elegant Back Bay area of Boston, filled with tall brick and stone rowhouses. C.F. could see he looked puzzled. "A fen was a smelly, old salt marsh. At low tide, it became mudflats until it was filled with dirt from Beacon Hill."

"Is that how Fenway Park got its name?" Mimi asked, meaning the famous baseball stadium in Boston.

"Yes," said Derian. "Buy me some peanuts and Cracker Jack . . ."

"We just had lunch!" said Aunt Emma.

As they crossed a bridge over the bluest water Christina had ever seen, she thought to ask, "Did women and blacks run in the Boston Marathon back then?"

"No way!" said Aunt Emma. "They weren't allowed to run. Those early marathoners and the people who put on the race probably never imagined the many different flavors of folks who would one day run in 'their' race. Or that thousands and thousands of runners would participate—instead of just a handful."

"I know where the first marathon was held," Grant

Back
Bay

Beacon
Hill

surprised everyone by saying.

"Where?" challenged C.F. and Derian together. Christina kept her mouth shut. She knew that Grant would not have made that comment unless he knew the facts. He had beat her often enough at *Trivial Pursuit, Jeopardy,* and other games for her to know better than to doubt him. Once Grant memorized something, he never forgot it.

Grant snuggled back into the seat contentedly. "In Greece. At the Olympics. They raced barefoot on sand between two poles. They could even push each other around, trip somebody, or kick sand in their face."

"Very good!" said Papa, with a big smile as the other boys, including Uncle Fritz, frowned at being upstaged by a seven-year-old.

"I know the rest of the story," said Priscilla, giving Grant a proud pat on the head. "The ordinary runners who took messages between the cities were the real athletes. One of those was Pheidippides. Supposedly, he ran 24 miles* over many hills one hot, summer day in 490 B.C. He was running from the Battle on the Plains of Marathon to deliver the message that the Athenian army had killed 6,400 Persian invaders. That was pretty good, considering the Greeks were outnumbered six to one!"

"It was," said Papa, who was a real history buff. "But

*38.6 kilometers

Beacon
Hill

Uncle Fritz's
House

that story may be more legend than truth. They said Pheidippides ran all that way in the hot sun, finally staggered his way into the chamber of rulers, and announced, 'Rejoice. We conquer!' Then, according to this legend, he dropped dead!"

"No matter how it really happened, we ended up with the word *marathon*," Priscilla finished.

"And, rejoice, we have finished ours!" said Uncle Fritz as he pulled down the long crushed oyster shell driveway to his Hopkinton farmhouse.

As everyone piled out of the SUV and stretched and headed for the house, Grant noticed movement in a large bush by the side of the house. He thought he heard footsteps patter away in the dirt, but he didn't see anything. Maybe he just had too many marathon legends lurking in his brain, he thought. He took a second glance, then shrugged his shoulders and bounded up the steps to catch up with the others. Maybe he could be a marathoner, he thought. Well, when his legs got longer.

Beacon Hill

Uncle Fritz's House

6 IT'S GREEK TO ME!

The next morning was Patriots' Day—the day of the big race! Everyone was up very early, especially Priscilla. The entire family gathered around the big oval-shaped kitchen table with the Lazy Susan built into the center. Everyone, except Priscilla.

"She ate earlier," Aunt Emma explained. "I think she's very excited about the race, but a little nervous."

"I know I would be," said Christina, reaching for the syrup to go on the humongous wild blueberry pancakes that Uncle Fritz and Papa had made on a griddle just outside on the screened porch. She gave the Lazy Susan a spin with the tips of her fingers and it went flying, as did butter, napkins, syrup, salt, pepper, and more. She was so embarrassed!

Instead of making fun of her, C.F. and Derian groaned

Uncle Fritz's
House

It's Patriot's
Day!

in understanding. "It happens to everyone sooner or later," they said.

They tossed the scattered items back on the Lazy Susan as if arranging playing pieces to start a board game. Christina was still red-faced. Maybe she just had pre-race jitters, she wondered, except she wasn't racing. However, she had always been an *empathetic* person. She used to say *sympathetic*, but her Mom said that was when you feel sorry for someone; empathetic was when you felt pain, or joy, or sadness, or whatever, just as strongly as another person did, even if what had caused the emotion had happened only to him or her.

Christina knew that if Priscilla beat the women's record, they all would be just as excited as she was. Priscilla suddenly bounded through the door, grinning broadly. "Well, I guess I'm as ready as I'll ever be," she said. She was wearing a pretty, bright pink shorts outfit.

"Hope you win!" said Christina.

Priscilla laughed, along with the rest of the family. Christina didn't get the joke, herself. "Oh, I'll never win!" Priscilla told her. "There are women who are much, much faster than I am or ever will be."

"Then why run?" Grant asked between bites of his own whopper pancakes.

Uncle Fritz's
House

It's Patriot's
Day!

"For the fun, the sport, the tradition," Priscilla explained. "Just to finish is a big deal," she said. "Of course, I hope to improve my time over the last marathon I ran. I'm not just running against the rest of the pack, you know. I'm running against myself."

Christina thought all that sounded very strange. She had assumed you ran to win, or at least come in second or third. But with 30,000 racers, she guessed maybe it *was* good to have some other motivation.

"You'll finish, sis," Derian said.

"We'll see," said Priscilla, and Christina saw what people call a "shadow of doubt" cross her face. Then she brightened up again. "If I do, you owe me a hot fudge sundae!" she told her younger brother.

"Now that's a deal I can make!" Derian promised.

On the way to Hopkinton Common, Uncle Fritz and Papa decided that as long as all four kids stayed together, they could be free from adult supervision for race day. Everyone was to meet at the bandstand in Boston Common at five that afternoon. Uncle Fritz gave C.F. and Derian each twenty dollars with a reminder not to spend it all in one place. Papa put Christina in charge of forty dollars for

Uncle Fritz's
House

The
Starting
Line

herself and Grant. He reminded her to be careful not to let Grant eat her out of house and pocket!

When the first Boston Marathon was run in 1897, William McKinley was president of the United States. Josiah Quincy was Mayor of Boston, which was already a town of almost half a million people. It was a city of horses, not cars. Most streets had never even been paved.

No wonder women didn't run in the race—why, they still wore corsets and petticoats and loads of other clothes! People had ice boxes, not refrigerators. They usually only bathed in a tin tub beside the fireplace, and that was only once a week. The bathroom was a little house out back, called an "outhouse" or "necessary house." It was, Christina thought, pretty much like the Dark Ages!

Christina had not learned all these new facts from Uncle Fritz. Instead, she had spent the entire evening reading in Uncle Fritz's home library. He had a whole shelf full of books just about the Boston Marathon. She also learned that centuries ago, a Greek water carrier named Spiridon Louis won the first modern Olympic Greek marathon.

Only 18 men had raced in the first Boston Marathon.

Uncle Fritz's
House

The
Starting
Line

Someone had simply hollered "GO!" to start, and then the racers just took off. Water carriers scampered alongside their favorite runner to hand him cups of water or toss water on him. During that first marathon, one runner even stopped a street-watering cart and asked the driver for a quick shower!

The leading runner in the first race got bogged down in a funeral procession. Later in the race, he even tangled with a couple of newfangled "electric" cars. In early races, most runners finished with bloody and blistered feet due to poor footwear. Winners usually just disappeared into an excited mob. There weren't even photos to put in the newspapers, just sketches drawn by artists of the race and the winner.

My, how times have changed, Christina pondered, as she stood on the edge of the Hopkinton town common. People were everywhere. They were from all over the world too! It seemed like half of them were reporters or television news camera operators. She saw CNN, NBC, CBS, ABC, FOX, and a whole alphabet soup of other networks. Good thing she had given Priscilla a good luck hug back at the house, because now, she could not have

Uncle Fritz's
House

The
Starting
Line

spotted her in this swarm of bodies.

When Christina saw the crowd of runners, it amazed her. She remembered Priscilla saying that runners had to qualify just to run in the Boston Marathon. Each runner needed a good time in a previous marathon. Numbers were assigned in the order of qualifying times. Those with the quickest times ran first. All that work just to be able to cross the starting line, she thought, let alone finish!

"I have an idea," said Derian. "I know a good place to see the start of the race. By the time Priscilla comes along, the pack will have thinned out some, and maybe we could follow alongside her for a little while!"

Christina thought that sounded exciting. She could pretend she was in the race. Grant looked down at his little short legs with a frown. "We'll help you," his sister promised. "Come on!"

Derian led the way through a gazillion onlookers, vendors selling everything from tee shirts to ice cream cones, and everyone else who had come out this sunny, but chilly Patriots' Day for the most famous marathon in the world.

This year, Christina thought, things were much different from the Revolutionary era. Most families had at least one car, usually two, or sometimes even three. Today,

Uncle Fritz's
House

The
Starting
Line

Hurrying to watch Priscilla!

names of the runners sounded like a roster from the United Nations. And there seemed to be as many runners as spectators, if the crowds of numbered athletes back at the common were any indication.

Christina held Grant's hand tightly as they scampered to keep up with Derian and C.F., who did not seem the least concerned whether or not they lost their Southern visitors. Soon, they reached the edge of a large field and stopped.

"This doesn't look like the start of the race to me," Christina complained, looking around at dried, brown, cornstalks taller than she was.

"Be patient," Derian said, with a grin.

Weaving like snakes, they curled through the cornfield until they came to the edge of the road. With a little practice, the kids could dig their toes into the dirt bank and see over the edge of the road bank and down toward the starting line.

"We can see the runners come by from here," said C.F. "Then we can cut across the field and catch up with them at one of our other secret spots."

Before Christina could complain about the dirt in her shoes and the straw in her hair, they heard the muffled crack of the starting gun.

"Aaaaannnnd, they're off!" cried C.F., as if it were a

Race
Starting Line

Race
Route

horse race.

Sure enough, they could soon easily hear, even feel, the thudding steps of the early runners coming toward them. Before too long, they were awash in the sound of slapping footsteps as forest after forest of legs passed by them.

Finally they saw the first women coming by. Then suddenly, Grant cried, "There she is!"

Priscilla and a number of other women ran by them in a blur. As she passed, they shouted "GO PRIS!" as loudly as they could. She turned just a little. Christina could see the surprised, confused look on her face, since she could not see the kids on the bank beneath her feet.

They all kept their eyes glued to her bright pink shorts and top as she went on down the road. Then a very strange thing happened. Priscilla disappeared!

7 OPTICAL ILLUSION

"Did you see that?" Derian asked. His voice grew wavery, as if he had seen something he could not believe.

"Yeah," said C.F., who sounded like he might cry. "Our sister just vanished—right before our eyes!"

Christina tried to calm them down, although she was pretty sure that she had seen the same thing. "Maybe it was just an optical illusion. You know, the bend in the road, or maybe we just lost her in the crowd."

Grant stood as tall as he could on the bank and peered hard down the track. "No," he said, seriously. "I saw it, too. She was on the road and, when everyone else turned, she just seemed to go straight and disappear. Except . . ."

"Except what?!" Derian asked.

Christina motioned for him to calm down. She could

Race
Route →

Where Did
She Go?

see that Grant was thinking hard to recall exactly what he had just witnessed. Something only he had seen from his low vantage point on the bankside.

Grant nodded his head slowly, as if he had convinced himself he was right. "Except," he said solemnly, "a hand grabbed her off the course. Right there." He pointed to a spot down the road, still rumbling with runners.

"It's the only explanation," Derian said, with a deep sigh.

"She wouldn't have just run off or quit," C.F. insisted. "She was too excited about this race, and she was doing good."

"Wouldn't someone running near her have noticed their fellow runner just disappeared right before their eyes?" Christina complained.

"They were probably just focused on the race," Derian said, "and moving so fast that they probably wouldn't have realized what they had seen. . .even if they had seen it," he added.

"Yeah," said C.F. "Sometimes runners do quit, you know. Or they step aside because they're sick,"

"Sick?" Grant repeated.

"Sure," said C.F. "You know, if they have to vomit."

"YUCK!" Grant and Christina cried together. They

Race
Route

Where Did
She Go?

each looked up at the steady river of runners and took a step backward, tumbling down the bank back into the corn rows.

C.F. looked disgusted. "Well, it happens," he said. "This is a hard, long race, you know. Some runners have even keeled over dead."

Suddenly, they all grew quiet. *Dead* was not a word they wanted to think about right now. Priscilla had, apparently, been kidnapped right before the eyes of hundreds of people, but it seemed that only they—four kids no one was likely to believe—had realized what had happened.

"I think we should go back to the house and tell your parents," Christina suggested urgently.

Derian shook his head. "They won't be there. They'll be headed for the finish line, and there's no way to contact them before we all meet up at five."

"We're pretty close to where Priscilla left the track," Christina said. "Maybe we should just head that way and see if we can catch up."

The kids looked at one another and nodded in agreement. "I know a shortcut!" said C.F., and he took off running through the cornfield in a direct line toward the curve where they had last seen Priscilla. The rest of the kids crashed after him.

Race
Route

Where Did
She Go?

"What kind of shortcut was that?" Christina grumbled, as soon as they reached the curve next to the Hopkinton woods. She was scratched up, tired, and dirty.

"Straight!" said C.F. triumphantly. "We got here quick, didn't we?"

"The shortest distance between two points *is* a straight line," Grant reminded his sister, as he looked up toward the treetops.

"Oh, keep your hypoteneus to yourself!" she grumbled, then added, "Look!"

Reaching out, she plucked a piece of torn fabric from a snapped branch. It was bright pink—the exact same color as Priscilla's running outfit!

8 KIDNAPPED!

The crowds of runners and race fans seemed very far away as the four kids went deeper into the Hopkinton woods. They neither saw nor heard anyone. Their cries of "Priscilla!" went unanswered. Pretty soon, they began to doubt themselves.

"Maybe we just imagined the whole thing?" C.F. suggested.

"Then how do you explain this?" demanded Christina, sticking out the swatch of pink fabric.

"Maybe it's a joke," said Derian.

"Not a very funny one," said Grant. "Who would want to snatch your sister off the course?"

The kids sat on the forest floor, already tired, hot, and dirty. Christina wondered if they were just looking for a way out of this mess before they got any deeper

Where Did She Go?

Priscilla's Path

45

into it.

At last, Derian spoke. "I can't imagine who'd want to hurt Priscilla," he said. "She's a fourth-grade teacher. How could she have any enemies?"

"Does she date?" Christina asked. "Who are her adult friends?"

"She doesn't date much, she runs," said C.F. "I think her adult friends are mostly just other teachers."

They didn't seem to be getting anywhere, so they headed for the road.

"I read somewhere that a man named Ronald McDonald won the second Boston Marathon in 1898," Derian said as they walked along.

"You mean like the hamburger chain clown?" asked Grant.

"No," said Derian. "I mean a real man who used to run to New York to practice for his races. Some people called him an eccentric."

"What's an eccentric?" C.F. asked.

"Someone who acts a little odd, or does things weird or differently," Derian explained. "At least other people think so."

"That could be anybody," suggested Christina.

"You don't mean Priscilla?" Grant asked. "She's not

Where Did
She Go?

Priscilla's
Path

centric."

"*Eccentric*, Grant," said Derian. "No, I don't think she'd pull a prank, or cheat and take a shortcut. But an eccentric person might grab her off the course, just to be silly or stupid, or to make a point."

"But what point?" Christina begged in exasperation. They had reached the road, which was lined with spectators. The runners were still coming full force.

"That's the million-dollar-question," said Derian. "And I don't have the final answer . . . yet," he added determinedly.

Suddenly, they heard more running, but it was coming from behind them. From out of the forest burst Prince, Uncle Fritz's hound dog.

"Hey, Prince!" Grant greeted him. He gave the tail-wagging, panting dog a scratch behind his floppy ears. "Didn't want to be left behind, huh?"

Christina bent down and looked closely at the dog. Stuck in one of the links of his collar chain was a small piece of paper. A message from home, she wondered. Or, maybe it was just a piece of litter. Gently, she pulled the rolled paper from the wriggling dog's collar.

"What is it?" asked Derian. He sounded gruff, like it was his dog and so he should have gotten to see what

Priscilla's Path

A Clue!

the paper was first.

Christina opened the note, read it, then looked up at the others. "It appears to me," she said smugly, "to be our first clue!" Prince wandered off as if he could care less.

Priscilla's Path   A Clue!

The boys finally read the first clue.

9 MARATHON MADNESS

"What does it say?" they all pleaded together. Derian tried to snatch the note away, but Christina held tightly to the scrap of paper.

"It says," she began, *"If you want to see your cousin Priscilla, you'd better be in good shape yourself. I am!"*

Derian said, "Let me see that!" and took the note. The boys gathered around to get a better look.

"What does that mean?" asked C.F.

"Who wrote it?" asked Grant.

"If we knew the answer to all those questions, we might know what happened to Priscilla," said Derian. "But I have an idea!" He pulled a map of the marathon race course from his pocket and spread it out. "If we have to be in good shape, then maybe the kidnapper means we'd better be able to run this race, too."

Priscilla's
Path

A Clue!

"Where are we on this map?" Christina asked.

Derian pointed to a spot not all that far from the start of the race. "We're here at Steven's Corner is my best guess," he said. He pointed to a spot up ahead. "Maybe if we can get to the South Framingham checkpoint, we can tell some race official what's going on and get some help."

It didn't look all that far, Christina thought, and they were "burning daylight" as Papa would say. "Well, what are we waiting for?"

The four kids took off, following the race course as closely as they could. The path went somewhat uphill after a while, so they were winded by the time they reached the checkpoint. However, it seemed the race officials were too busy keeping up with the steady stream of runners to mess with a handful of unruly kids. The kids tried being polite, then urgent, and then demanding, but all their methods did them no good. No one seemed to believe the story of their sister and cousin being snatched from the Boston Marathon.

They were mostly ignored, until one busy man asked, "Did you say Priscilla?"

"Yes!" they agreed eagerly.

Without taking his eyes off his clipboard, the man reached around to a message board and plucked off an envelope. "This message is for a Priscilla," he said,

A Clue!

Race
Route

handing it to the nearest hand, which was Derian's.

"Thanks," Derian said, and the kids ducked out of the chaos before the man changed his mind about giving them the message clearly intended for Priscilla.

"Open it!" the rest of the kids demanded as soon as they were back out of the crowd.

Derian looked at the envelope. It had Priscilla's name written on it in big, block letters. To him, it seemed very strange that his sister would get a message during the Boston Marathon. There certainly had to be more than one Priscilla in the race, since there was no last name shown.

"Open it!" the kids demanded once more.

Derian tore the envelope open and a piece of paper fell out. Quickly he read the message:

YOU WILL NOT BE
FINISHING THE RACE.
YOU DIDN'T LET MY
SON FINISH.

A Clue!

Race
Route

"Wow!" said Christina. "This clue sounds much more ominous."

"I wish you'd stop calling them *clues*," said Derian. "One was just a note on a dog's collar, and this one was just a message to my sister, that's all." He looked confused and dejected.

"It just makes sense!," insisted Christina. "That's all we have to go on right now. This seems like a mystery to me, and these stupid little notes are the only clues we have to solve it."

Derian and C.F. gave each other a resigned look. They figured they'd better not argue. They knew that Christina's and Grant's grandmother Mimi wrote mysteries for kids and that her own kids and grandkids often got into hot water trying to solve them. Now *they* were stuck in one.

Everyone was silent. No one disagreed, but no one knew exactly what to do either. They stood there quietly while the world around them marched on like a festive parade.

"I know," said Grant. "Let's look at your map again." They spread the race course map out on the ground. "Whoever took Priscilla might be at least following the race course, so let's see if we can get one step ahead. Maybe then we will see Priscilla and her kidnapper come by."

A Clue!

Race
Route

"But he said she wouldn't finish the race," said C.F.

"Yes," Grant agreed, "but he didn't really say she wouldn't run any of it."

"Grant's right," said Derian. "We aren't getting anywhere standing here. If we go on ahead, maybe we will see Priscilla somewhere on—or off—the course."

The others nodded in agreement until Christina made a suggestion. "We'll never get ahead unless we get a ride."

Before they knew what was happening, Derian was talking to a police officer who was just getting into her patrol car. "We got separated from our parents," he told her. The other kids could see his fingers crossed behind his back. "Can we get a ride with you up to City Hall?"

The officer looked exasperated, but she seemed to be too rushed to think much about the request. "Oh, okay," she said. "Get in the back seat, but hurry up about it."

In split seconds the kids had piled into the back of the patrol car and were speeding down a side lane alongside the race course.

"Hey, this is a great way to see the race!" said C.F.

"Hush!" whispered Christina. "Derian just told a big, giant fib."

"But a necessary one?" Derian responded.

"I guess so," Christina agreed. "But it could still get us

Race
Route

City
Hall

in a lot of trouble."

"Not as much trouble as *that*!" said C.F., pushing all the kids down beneath the windows.

"What's going on?" the officer asked from the front seat.

"We dropped something," C.F. called up to her, then pointed for the others to peek out the window. There on the corner stood Aunt Emma, Uncle Fritz, Mimi, and Papa! Fortunately, their backs were to the patrol car. They were watching the race, probably watching for Priscilla, Christina figured. Uncle Fritz was waving the runners on, his arms swinging wildly.

The kids sat back up after the car moved ahead. "Maybe we should have stopped and told them what was going on," C.F. said.

"Probably," said Derian, "but we would be wasting time with explanations . . . and we don't even have any."

It was too late anyway. The officer stopped the car and called out, "City Hall! Good luck finding your parents."

"Thanks for the ride," the kids said and gave her parting waves.

"Now what?" asked Christina.

"Let's just start walking," Derian suggested.

The course was hillier here. They walked quickly and

silently, dodging onlookers, and keeping an eye out for Priscilla. Suddenly, up ahead, they spotted something pink! "Hurry!" Christina cried. They tried to speed up, but the spectators were too thickly clustered along the roadside.

Christina kept a close eye on the pink shorts as she sped ahead. The others tried to keep up. As she jogged, she thought about what she'd been reading about early Boston Marathons, because it kept popping in her head. In 1900, the *Boston Herald* had proclaimed, "No weaklings will be permitted to start in the marathon tomorrow."

As she breathed heavily, Christina thought how much she felt like a weakling. She thought of the long-ago runners who had worked as blacksmiths, team horse drivers, miners, shopkeepers, and at other back-breaking jobs which must have helped them with their endurance during the race. No wonder some of them were called *braggadocios*. They probably had *earned* the right to brag, she thought!

Christina glanced behind her, and seeing the others trailing farther behind in her wake, she slowed down her pace. The pink shorts vanished from her line of sight. Derian caught up with her. "Now you know why they call this Heartbreak Hill," he said.

City Hall

Heartbreak Hill

C.F. pulled up short, holding his side with both hands. "Got a stitch," he complained.

Grant was the tagalong. He grinned widely as he approached the others. They wondered why, until they watched him pass by them merrily. "Beatcha!" he shouted.

The kids raced after him, but it was no use. The pink shorts had vanished.

10 TATER PEELER AND KITCHEN RATS!

The kids witnessed loads of curious sights as they tried to keep up with the race crowd, both contenders and families, friends, and strangers cheering them on. One rather hefty woman trudged after her son, constantly calling, "Claypool, honey, hurry up!" Claypool ignored her.

Another racer (last name Peeler) had sewed his nickname inside quotation marks on his jersey so fans would know his full name was "TATER" PEELER. Another racer had his hometown–MUDDY, ILLINOIS: POPULATION 100–emblazoned on his shirt.

A group of female racers each had the tag "Kitchen Rats" scrawled on the back of their shorts. Christina figured that meant they worked in a restaurant.

One lady racer had embroidered her name on her shirt with beautiful spring flowers. "What an unusual type font,"

Heartbreak
Hill

Race
Route

Christina said, explaining to the others that a font was a family of letters all created in the same style by one artist.

"You're just a font of information," Derian complained. "Except when it comes to our current mystery."

"You mean *fount*," Christina said irritably, knowing he was right.

It was true. They were pretty much bombing out. As the racers thinned out along the course, so did their ideas. And their energy. Suddenly C.F. had a brilliant idea. "Let's catch the bus to town!" he suddenly suggested.

"What good will that do?" asked Grant.

At first, C.F. didn't seem to be sure, but he was sure he didn't want to run, walk, trot, or otherwise pound the pavement any longer. Actually, his logic wasn't half bad. "Well," he said. "If we think we can still see Priscilla, or at least her pink shorts, then she's still in the race. If she's going all the way to town, then we might as well get there ahead of her and perhaps help her and catch the guy who kidnapped her."

No one really argued because they were tired, too. "Okay," said Derian, "but let's take the T instead."

"What's the T?" asked Christina.

"The subway," C.F. explained. "We can take the T to the Common and walk from there."

Heartbreak
Hill

Race
Route

"The common what?" Grant asked.

Derian and C.F. laughed. "The Boston Common!" they said together.

Christina did not laugh back. She cleared her throat. "The Boston Common is America's oldest public park," she explained to her brother. "It's about 50 acres* of open land right in the middle of Boston. It was once used as pasture by the townspeople for their cattle. The Common was originally owned by William Blackstone, who came to Boston in 1622. It was also used as a training field for soldiers during the Revolutionary War, but the British army also used it for a camp. People have been hung there, duels have been fought there, and parties and fireworks were also held sometimes."

"How'd you know all that?" C.F. asked, incredulous.

Derian quickly reached around behind Christina and grabbed the blue booklet she had tucked in her back pocket. "She cheated!" he shouted. "She's got a copy of the Freedom Trail guide, and she's been reading it."

Christina laughed. "That's not cheating! That's research! I picked it up at the Common in Hopkinton." she said. "That was also smart because it's coming in handy!" The two continued their spirited argument as they all boarded the T and headed for downtown Boston. Once

*19 hectares

The "T"
To Boston

Boston Common

aboard the train, they were glad to sit down and rest.

Everyone was quiet. The subway was empty except for a man in a dark, hooded jacket near the front of the car. When he got off at the next stop, he dropped a plastic capsule on the car floor. Derian jumped up to grab it, but before he could shout out that he had lost something, the man was gone.

Derian sat back down beside the other kids and forced the plastic capsule open. A folded piece of pink paper popped out, accordion-style. They looked at one other. This time, Grant grabbed the clue first and read aloud:

LET THE FREEDOM
TRAIL RING!

The "T"
To Boston

Boston
Common

11 RED HERRINGS

As they continued their ride on the T, the kids forgot to look out of the window at the early Boston spring scenery. Instead they argued over what the clue meant.

"And," as Christina put it, "why did that guy follow us on the T? Is he trying to lead us *toward* something, or *away* from something?"

"You mean like a red herring?" Derian asked.

"He's trying to lead us toward fish?" C.F. asked, puzzled.

"No," said Derian. "A red herring is a false clue. Maybe he's trying to get us off track."

"The subway track?" asked Grant, holding onto the side of his seat tightly.

Christina giggled. "The mystery track," she said. "And you know, if he *is* trying to lead us astray, then that means that we *were* on the right track following Priscilla down the

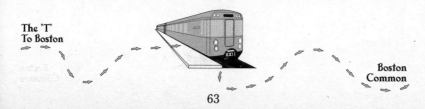

The "T"
To Boston

Boston
Common

race course."

"Yeah," Derian said. "But if this clue's not a red herring, then he might be trying to lead us *to* Priscilla."

"Why would he do that if he's trying to kidnap her?" C.F. pondered.

"Good question," Derian replied.

"We have lots of good questions, but no good answers," observed Grant.

"Look, I don't think we have any choice but to follow the clues we've got for now," Christina said, "even if they *do* get us in big trouble later."

The boys didn't look like they liked the sound of that idea, but they offered no argument. "Freedom Trail it is then," said Derian.

"Freedom Trail," said C.F.

"Freedom Trail," parroted Grant.

Christina planted her fist into her palm determinedly. "Freedom Trail," she muttered ominously.

The T brought them very near to the start of the 2.5 mile (4.02 kilometer) Freedom Trail at the corner of Boston Common. The walking trail took tourists all around the historic sites of downtown Boston, Beacon Hill, and the

The "T"
To Boston

Boston
Common

Setting off on the Freedom Trail!

North End, where Paul Revere had once lived.

"I have an idea," Grant said. "As we get to each site, why don't we stop and think about why the kidnapper might be leading us there. Maybe there's only one site that really matters!"

Christina put her arm around her brother. "That's a great idea, Grant," she said encouragingly. The other boys started following the bright red strip of bricks that marked the trail.

"I can tell you that we are going to be very tired in a very little while," Derian warned them.

"Would you rather go back and run the race?" C.F. asked, teasingly.

"No way!" the other three kids agreed.

"Let's march on!" Derian added energetically, and off they went.

Their next stop was the Massachusetts State House. Christina pulled out her blue guide and read, "This is the oldest building on Beacon Hill. It was finished in 1798 and houses the Hall of Flags and the House and Senate Chambers."

"I heard they also once tried pirates in court here!" said Derian.

C.F. stared up thoughtfully at the beautiful building with

its white columns and glistening gold dome. "A red flag," he said softly.

"Probably," agreed Derian. "There's probably a red flag in the Hall of Flags."

C.F. shook his head animatedly. "No," he said, "that's not what I mean. I mean we should look closely for a *red flag*."

"Is that anything like a red herring?" Grant asked, obviously puzzled, since he did not see any red flags or fish anywhere, only the red bricks of the trail.

"Sort of," said Christina. "I think C.F. means that we should continue to look for clues, or for anything that looks odd or out of place—a 'red flag' that something's wrong."

"But how will we know when we see a red flag if it's not really a red flag?" Grant asked, more puzzled than ever.

"That's what makes this mystery so hard to solve," Derian said. "We won't know what we're looking for until we see it."

C.F. laughed. "Oh, that makes lots of sense!" he said, swinging around the street sign pole. "Got it now, Grant?"

Grant just shook his head. "Not really."

"Maybe we'd better head for the next site on the Freedom Trail," Christina suggested.

"Amen, sister!" said Derian, looking both ways quickly, and then dashing across the street.

"What does that mean?" Grant asked.

Christina glanced down at the guide book. "It means that the next site is a church," she said, racing after Derian. C.F. took one more swing around the pole and followed the others with Grant.

At the corner of Park and Tremont Streets, the kids strained their necks to look up at the tall steeple of a church that was almost 200 years old.

"I know what happened here," Grant said.

"What?" asked C.F., obviously very doubtful that a stranger to Boston would know anything about the historic Park Street Church.

Grant stood tall and said, "On July 4, 1831, the song *America* (you know, 'My country 'tis of thee') was first sung here."

"We know the song," said Derian, "but how did you know that tiny bit of trivia?"

"I read the sign!" Grant answered in a teasing voice. He pointed to the historic marker in front of the church.

The rest of the kids groaned.

"Well, *I* know that William Lloyd Garrison delivered a big speech against slavery here in 1829," said C.F. "So there!"

freedom
Trail

Park Street
Church

"And how did YOU know that?" Christina asked.

C.F. doubled over in laughter. "I read the *other* side of the historic marker!" he said.

The rest of the kids groaned even louder.

"We're getting nowhere," said Derian. "Let's try next door."

Next door was the old Granary Burying Ground. Even in the middle of a sunny spring day, the cemetery seemed dark, foreboding, and spooky. The kids wandered silently among the tombstones, that looked as if they were tousled by the wind.

"Hey! John Hancock was buried here!" said C.F., peering closely at the ancient words carved into one stone. "Wasn't he the guy who . . ." he began.

"Yeah, he sure was," Christina interrupted.

"Who what?" asked Grant, wondering if his sister knew how to read minds.

"Who signed the Declaration of Independence," said C.F.

"You'll study that in school soon," Christina said. "But I'll bet your teacher might not tell you that John Hancock might not be buried here after all. After he was buried, grave robbers cut off the hand he signed the Declaration with . . . and his body may have been moved too, sometime later."

"What is a granary anyway?" Grant asked, deciding to ignore his sister's gruesome trivia.

Park Street
Church

Granary Burial
Ground

Suddenly, Derian popped out from behind a large tombstone and shouted, "BOO!" The other kids screamed.

"A granary was where the colonists kept grain," he shouted at them.

The kids stopped and turned around.

"Well, that's food for thought," C.F. said.

"Don't be so pun-y," warned Derian.

The kids should have laughed, but instead, they stared past Derian as if they really did see a ghost. "What is it?" he asked nervously, slowly turning around to see what had caused their mouths to hang open so wide.

When he turned around to look, he gasped. On the pointy top of one of the wrought iron fence posts hung a scrap of paper. Quickly and quietly, the kids drew closer until they could read the writing scrawled on the flapping square of pink.

FOLLOW THE ~~YELLOW~~ RED BRICK ROAD! WHAT YOU'RE LOOKING FOR IS QUITE A LOAD!

Park Street Church

Granary Burial Ground

The kids stood still thinking quietly for a few moments. At last, Christina spoke. "Well, that certainly must mean to keep going along the trail."

"Yeah," said Derian, "but what about that second line? It sounds like Priscilla is not running on her own anymore. It sounds like he's carrying her."

No one spoke for a minute.

"Let's not jump to conclusions," said Christina. She didn't like the sound of the clue either, but she also didn't want to scare the other kids, or even believe anything bad could really happen to Priscilla.

"Then let's jump back on the trail," C.F. said.

"I'm ready to get out of this creepy place," Grant agreed. And without another word, the foursome wove their way among the tombstones back onto the sunny sidewalk and sped down the street.

They never saw the figure in the shadows following slowly behind them.

12 THIS IS NO TEA PARTY!

The kids hurried past a statue of Benjamin Franklin, who seemed to give them a mysterious and perhaps disapproving look as they passed by. Christina noticed that they were now on School Street, where the Boston Latin School was opened in 1635—a very long time ago, she thought! America's first public school was still in operation, but now it was at another location.

She would have loved to have stopped at the Old Corner Bookstore, where famous authors such as Charles Dickens, Ralph Waldo Emerson, Henry Wadsworth Longfellow, Henry David Thoreau, and others had once dawdled. Maybe even the author of her favorite book, *Little Women*, Louisa May Alcott had come here! Just the thought gave Christina cold chills! She wanted to be a writer just like her grandmother. Her favorite thing was to go on school visits

Ben Franklin's
Statue

Old State
House

73

with Mimi. Sometimes kids asked Mimi to autograph their books. Other times she autographed their milk cartons, tee shirts, or even their arms!

Derian, the leader of the pack at the moment, didn't even slow down at the famous Old South Meeting House, the starting point of the even more famous Boston Tea Party, when angry colonists rebelled against British taxation by dumping chests of tea from British ships into the harbor in protest.

Who could blame them, thought Christina, as she jumped the curb to try to keep up. Taxes pay for public services, but the British just got too greedy. And, of course, this rebellion led to the Revolutionary War and America becoming its very own country.

She was so caught up in her historical daydreaming that she almost missed the Old State House. It was a large and grand building that Christina recalled from her brochure. The Declaration of Independence was read to the colonists from its elegant balcony in 1776. In fact, if she remembered correctly, this was even the backdrop for the Boston Massacre!

"Oomph!"

Christina didn't know who was more startled when she ran into the back of the boys as they stood huddled in the

Old State House

Boston Massacre Site

middle of a traffic island surrounded by cobblestones.

"Excuuuuse us for standing!" Derian hollered to Christina. "You almost knocked us into a bus, princess!"

"Well, oops. I was just remembering that the Boston Massacre took place here!" Christina gushed excitedly.

Grant was all excited. "This is where the Boston Massacre took place?" he said. "What's a massacre?"

Derian turned toward Grant to answer his questions.

"It was right here in this exact spot that the patriots and redcoats clashed for the first time. Five men were killed," Derian said. "The first to die was a black man named Crispus Attucks. He was the first casualty of the American Revolution."

Christina explained further that the horrific event outraged the colonists so much that they were determined to start a rebellion. "The tragedy even turned some Tories, people who still sympathized with the British crown, into patriots."

"Well *we're* going to be massacred next if we don't get out of this traffic soon," Derian insisted, muttering under his breath about clumsy girl cousins. The others agreed by following him down Congress Street toward a very large building surrounded by crowds, clowns, balloons, artists, craftspeople, and all sorts of wonderful smells.

Old State
House

Boston
Massacre
Site

"What's that?" Grant asked.

"Faneuil Hall," said C.F. "It's known as the Cradle of Liberty," he added, "and it's also a great place to eat! Just look at all these neat Quincy Market eateries."

"Yeah, let's do," said Grant. "I'm starving. This mystery solving is no tea party!"

"I'm famished, too," said Derian.

Christina put her hands on her hips and stomped her foot hard. The boys stopped and stared at her as she glared at them.

"What's wrong?" Derian asked her. He thought she looked like an angry teacher.

"How can you guys think about food when poor Priscilla is who-knows-where with who-knows-who who has who-knows-what plans and who-knows-when he might do something bad?"

In spite of themselves, the boys laughed, but stopped suddenly, when they saw that Christina was close to tears.

"You're right," Derian agreed. "But it might be a long day and even longer night, and I don't think it would be so awful to grab a quick bite."

"Even detectives have to eat," C.F. said.

Grant just stood there rubbing his stomach with a solemn "I'm gonna starve to death right here, sis" look on

Boston Massacre
Site

Faneuil
Hall

his face. In spite of herself, Christina heard her tummy rumble and her mouth felt dry.

"Ok," she said, handing Grant five dollars. "A *quick* bite."

As soon as she said the word "quick," the boys took off running in different directions. Christina headed through the crowd herself and they soon gathered back together at a table under an enormous old tree. It *was* good to sit down for a minute, she admitted to herself.

Christina had bought fresh-squeezed lemonade and a cup of Boston Baked Beans with a thick slice of Boston Brown Bread. Derian had already gobbled half his hotdog and was devouring some sort of soup. C.F. was chowing down on a hamburger, and Grant was stuffing french fries into his mouth as fast as he could.

Christina observed the boys' eating habits with thinly disguised disgust. "You cretins are grossing me out," she said. "Who taught you all manners? Anybody?"

Grant ignored his sister's ranting, as usual.

"How's your soup?" Grant asked Derian. It smelled wonderful!

"It's not soup," he said, "it's chowdah!"

When Grant looked puzzled, C.F. translated: "*Chowder*!"

Faneuil Hall

Quincy Market

Christina nodded with understanding. She had tasted chowder before. "Well, while we're sitting here, let's recap where we are."

"We're at Fnnlll Hlll," Grant mumbled, his mouth full of food, cheeks poking out like a nut-stuffed squirrel.

"I know we're at Faneuil Hall!" Christina said with a sigh. "I mean where we are on the mystery of what has happened to Priscilla?"

"We're nowhere," said C.F.

"Nah, we have clues," Derian said in disagreement.

"But the clues are taking us nowhere," C.F. grumbled back.

"*No*, they're taking us down the Freedom Trail," Christina said, running her finger down the red line in her brochure. "But to where and what and when and why?"

"If we knew all that we could solve the mystery right now," said Derian.

"Well if we just sit here yakking all afternoon, we'll never solve the mystery or find Priscilla," C.F. said.

"But if we get up we'll have to walk four million more miles," moaned Grant, whose legs, of course, were shorter than everyone else's.

Christina got up and went to throw her trash in a nearby garbage can. "We'll walk slower," she promised her little

brother. Then, suddenly, she seemed to change her mind. "Or faster!" she cried.

"What's wrong?" Derian asked, noting the urgency in her voice.

Christina whipped around and grabbed a pink scrap of paper from the flip top of the garbage can lid. "Another clue! You know, the only way these clues could keep popping up like this is if the kidnapper was around *here* somewhere."

Every head at their table began to look left and right at the crowds that surrounded them. Grant even looked under the table, which made C.F. laugh. But there was no one to see, at least no one they thought looked like a kidnapper–whatever that looked like. The only pink in sight was the clue, which Christina read:

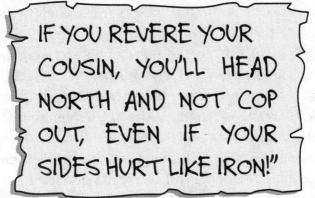

IF YOU REVERE YOUR COUSIN, YOU'LL HEAD NORTH AND NOT COP OUT, EVEN IF YOUR SIDES HURT LIKE IRON!"

Quincy Market

Freedom Trail

Derian rubbed his crew cut scalp. Beads of sweat started to form on his forehead. Christina didn't know if he was flushed, tired, sick, worried, or all four.

"What's wrong?" she asked.

Derian sat back down on the bench with a thud. "Give me your guidebook," he said. Christina handed it right over and he began to thumb through it. "Just like I thought," he said.

"Thunk what?" asked C.F., hanging over Derian's shoulder.

Derian shrugged him off. "Not thunk, you moron, thought."

"Forget about all that!" said Grant. "Tell us what you thinked."

Christina groaned loudly. "Not thunk, not thinked, you ninnies . . ." But before she could continue correcting the boys' grammar, Derian interrupted her.

"See!" He yanked the book open and pointed to a page. "This bad guy's really pulling our chain. I think he wants to wear us down by making us walk the entire Freedom Trail. I think the word *revere* in the clue means our next stop is Paul Revere's House. And *north* means the Old North Church, the next stop on the trail. And *cop* means Copp's Hill Burying Ground!"

Grant groaned. "Not another cemetery!"

Derian ignored him and continued. "And *iron* means Old Ironsides, the *USS Constitution*."

"Well, what's so bad about that?" asked Christina. "If the clues are leading us where we need to go, then it's great that he told us in this clue, and that you figured it all out."

"I don't think it's so great," Derian said. "The next three places are pretty close, but then the Freedom Trail goes all the way over to the Charleston Navy Yard, across the Charles River. We'll be exhausted. It'll be getting dark soon, we may be late to the bandstand, and we don't even know if this is a wild goose chase or not."

Unfortunately, Christina could see what he was getting at. Gingerly, she picked up the pink scrap of paper. "But what choice do we have except to press on?" she asked.

"None," said Derian. "Priscilla's counting on us. We won't let her down. But time is of the essence, you know. The day's rushing by as fast as the race. If it gets dark . . ."

". . . all hope may be lost," Christina finished dejectedly.

One by one, they quietly tossed the rest of the trash

Freedom
Trail

Paul
Revere's
House

in the garbage and soberly trudged single-file back down Freedom Trail. It seemed they were prisoners of the trail and the string of clues until they found their schoolteacher cousin and sister . . . dead or alive.

Freedom
Trail

Paul
Revere's
House

13 ONE IF BY LAND, TWO IF BY SEA

It seemed that there was nothing to do but to keep dragging onward over the often lumpy sidewalk of the red brick trail. Tourist traffic was pretty light; Christina figured most people were focused on the race today. In spite of being tired and worried about Priscilla, she couldn't help but be really excited when they came to the home of Paul Revere.

Built around 1680, his house was the oldest building in downtown Boston, and it really looked it! Christina remembered studying the famous patriot in her social studies class last year.

"Wow!" said Grant, looking up at the rickety building. "So this is where the famous 'Midnight Ride of Paul Revere' started."

"One if by land and two if by sea, and all that jazz,"

Paul Revere's House

Old North Church

said C.F.

"That's right," said Christina. "And then the first battle of the Revolution was fought at Lexington Green."

Derian looked up at the house thoughtfully. "You know, I think we need to go inside since the clue mentioned this place especially."

The other kids nodded in agreement and walked through the gate of the fence that surrounded the courtyard of the old house. It was quiet and no one seemed to be around at the moment. Christina could easily imagine herself living back during the Revolutionary era in Boston. It must have been exciting, she thought, and a little scary with all the spying and skirmishes going on all around.

When they went through the small back door, they found themselves in a dingy kitchen room that smelled of stale smoke. "This isn't too glamorous," said Derian.

"It wouldn't have been," Christina reminded him. "Remember, these famous patriots that we study in school weren't old and gray back then when they did their famous stuff—they were just regular guys like brothers and dads—at least that's what our teacher told us."

"I never thought about it that way," said Derian, screwing his nose up at the smoky smell. "So any ordinary person could get to be a famous hero, I guess."

Paul Revere's
House

Old North
Church

As they began climbing a tiny, narrow staircase to the upstairs, Christina turned and said to him, "I think Priscilla is counting on that."

Upstairs were more small rooms and a collection of the beautiful silversmith work Paul Revere was known for. C.F. really admired the oversized silverware, large goblets, bowls, tea services, and other items that were as shiny as if they had been crafted yesterday, not hundreds of years ago. "I wish I could give my Mom one of these for Christmas," he said wistfully.

"Better save up," said Derian. "They look expensive."

"Better rob a bank!" C.F. suggested. "They're priceless!"

"Better not!" said Christina. "You know what happened to those Brinks robbers," she added reminding them of the famous Boston bank robbery that Mimi had told her about one time.

Suddenly, a large man appeared in the tiny doorway. He was dressed in Revolutionary era garb, including large-buckle boots and a tricorn hat. The kids gasped. Just for a moment, they wondered if the ghost of Paul Revere was standing before them. But this ghost was too loud to be dead!

"What are you kids doing up here?" he demanded gruffly. "Don't you know you're supposed to buy a ticket to

Paul Revere's
House

Old North
Church

get in here?" He began to shoo them down another tiny twisting-turning staircase.

"We didn't see anyone," Derian told him, as he tripped hurriedly down the last few steps.

"We didn't mean to sneak inside," Christina added. "We were just looking for . . ." Her voice trailed off as he whisked the back door open and escorted them out into the courtyard and back through the fence gate.

"Wow! Was that getting the bum's rush?" asked Grant.

"What's that?" C.F. asked, puzzled.

"It's just something Papa says," Grant explained. "I don't know what it means either, but that sure felt like it."

As they hit the Freedom Trail yet again, Christina reminded them that they hadn't found a clue inside anyway, so they may just as well be on their way. "Besides," she said, "the rest of the Paul Revere story can be found right here!"

"Here" was the Old North Church, the oldest church building in Boston, that was built in 1723. Once again, Christina had that eerie feeling of being transported back in time. The church was made of beautiful red brick, and the steeple shone bright white against the blue sky.

"See up there," said Derian. The kids all craned their necks to look up at the bell tower on top of the church.

Paul Revere's
House

Old North
Church

Watching for a signal.

"That's where the church sexton hung the two lanterns to warn Paul Revere and others about which direction the British would come from that night."

"It was a cool way to leave a clue," C.F. admitted.

"I wish *we* could find another clue," moaned Christina, opening one of the large doors to the church and going inside. She was surprised to see that the church was still used for regular services, even after all these years. However, on this busy race day, it was cool and quiet inside. As she sat down in one of the box pews, she could swear that all she could hear were her heart beating and a clock ticking. When she turned to look up at the old clock, she was shocked to see the curtains behind it part and an arm thrust through and begin to move the clock hands.

"What's up?" Grant asked, looking up quizzically at the clock himself.

"I don't know," Christina whispered. "I guess they do have to set the clock now and then," she pondered. But just before the arm disappeared back through the slit in the curtain, the person reached down and tucked a pink note behind the hour hand of the clock.

"Did you see that?!" the other boys squealed. They had come in the church just in time to witness their nemesis leaving what looked like the next clue for them! Without

Paul Revere's
House

Old North
Church

another word, Derian and C.F. dashed back out into the vestibule and scampered up the steps to the clock gallery.

The next thing Christina saw was Derian and C.F. leaning down precariously to try to reach the clock hands. When they couldn't, Derian grabbed his brother by the heels and hung him over the balcony.

"Hey, you guys be careful up there!" Christina cried. But before she could fuss at them further, C.F. grabbed the pink note. As Derian hoisted him back up, the note slipped from his fingers and fluttered down into the sanctuary like a pink butterfly. Grant ran through the maze of pews and grabbed it.

"No fair!" C.F. cried down to him. "Wait for us! We found it first."

But Grant and his sister couldn't wait. Christina had caught up with Grant by clambering over the low walls that divided the pews—something her Mom would have thrown a tantrum about if she had seen her! Even as they heard their cousins thundering back down the staircase, she and Grant read the clue:

Old North
Church

Freedom
Trail

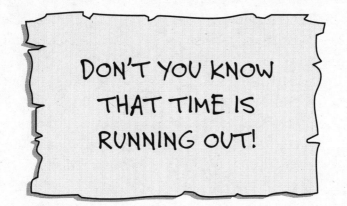

DON'T YOU KNOW
THAT TIME IS
RUNNING OUT!

Old North
Church

freedom
Trail

14 TIME IS RUNNING OUT!

"Well, that's sure discouraging," the boys muttered when they got back down to the sanctuary and read the clue for themselves. They were so distressed that they forgot to be angry at Grant and Christina for reading the note first.

Christina was very quiet. Once more, all she could hear were her heartbeat and the clock ticking very evenly. "You know," she said suddenly. "If you guys went UP the staircase to the clock gallery at the same time as Grant and I were still looking at that arm, then how did he get back DOWN and escape without you both passing him?"

Now everyone was quiet. It was a good question with no easy answer. "Ghost?" suggested Grant.

"Secret passage?" wondered C.F. aloud.

Old North Church

Freedom Trail

"He could have flown off the steeple," said Derian.

"And just exactly how could he have done that?" Christina asked.

"I don't know," said Derian, waving a blue flier in her face, "but this brochure says that some guy did just that in 1757. Three times, Christina!"

"Well, if the bad guy was here in the church with us," Grant pondered, "then where is Priscilla?"

Christina brushed her hair off her forehead. "That's a mystery, all right," she said. "And it's one that really worries me."

"Aw, everything worries you, Christina," Derian groused.

"And nothing seems to worry you, buster," Christina snarled back at him.

"Temper, temper, children," said C.F.

Grant laughed.

"No tantrums allowed. We gotta work together," C.F. cautioned.

"We've got to work faster is what we have to do," said Christina. "I mean, just look!" She waved her hand toward the windows. Outside, it was growing dusky in the late afternoon sun of early spring. They only had a couple of hours of daylight left.

Old North
Church

Freedom
Trail

Suddenly, Derian took off running. From a dark corner near the front doors, he grabbed an armful of something and dashed back. At their feet he plopped down a batch of old rollerblades and a scooter. "Maybe these will help?"

"Some kids must have tried to wear those to church," Grant said.

"Looks like they didn't get away with it," said C.F.

"Well, I don't see why we can't borrow them for a little while," said Derian.

"You mean steal?" asked Christina. "From a church?!"

"I said borrow," Derian insisted. "We can return them later."

Without another word, the kids switched and swapped skates until each had a pair that fit, more or less, except for Grant, who happily grabbed the scooter. Just as they were rolling toward the door, a minister in black robes came inside the church. He rubbed his eyes hard as if he were seeing things.

"Hey, you kids," he cried. "Don't you know those things aren't allowed in . . ." But before he could finish his sentence, the kids rolled right past him.

"Sorry," said Christina.

"Excuse us!" said C.F.

"Pardon me, parson," said Derian.

"Pray for uuuuuusssssss!" squealed Grant, as he bumped bumped bumped down the church steps and back out onto the Freedom Trail.

In just a couple of bumpy blocks, they found themselves at Copp's Burying Ground. Christina couldn't help but think how the rows of rounded-top slate tombstones looked like rows of books. *Books of the dead,* she thought sadly. She rubbed her fingers in the holes musket balls had made when the slate tombstones had been used by the British soldiers for target practice.

"So this is where they bury Boston's police officers?" Grant asked, reading the Copp's sign.

"Huh?" said Derian, rolling unsteadily across the lumpy ground.

"You know—the cops," Grant said.

The other kids laughed. Grant folded his arms across his chest, curled his upper lip up to his nose and squinted his eyes. Christina knew that was his body language for "You've hurt my feelings" and "Don't make

Freedom
Trail

Copp's Hill
Burying
Ground

fun of me." She also knew he might actually cry if she didn't step in and save the day. "It's ok, Grant," she said to her brother. "It's Copp's–like a man's name, not like a police cop."

"Oh," said Grant dejectedly. He dropped his arms and decided to let the matter drop as well.

"Well, there could be some cops buried here," C.F. said. "This old burying ground was the last stop for North End Bostoners of all types, like merchants, artisans, and craftspeople. They even hung pirates from the gallows and people would gather in their boats below to watch."

"You're starting to sound too much like a teacher," Derian criticized his brother.

C.F. propped against one of the tombstones. "Well, I don't care," he said. "I want to be a teacher–like Priscilla."

Christina had been reading one of the old historic markers. "Thousands of free blacks were also buried here," she told the others. "I know that Boston was listed on the Underground Railroad routes."

"Then where are the tracks?" asked Grant.

"It wasn't a real railroad," Christina explained. "It was a string of safe houses where slaves could stay

Freedom
Trail

Copp's Hill
Burying
Ground

while escaping from the South to the North and their freedom."

"And this is also the place where the British aimed their cannons on Charlestown during the Battle of Bunker Hill," said Derian. He pointed out across the landscape to the horizon. The other kids just stared.

"You mean we've got to get all the way over there?" asked Christina. From the top of this hill she could see that "over there" was across a body of water where Bunker Hill stood. The ship the *USS Constitution* was docked in the Charlestown Navy Yard.

"How will we ever get there in time?" she moaned.

"In time for what?" Grant asked.

"I don't know," Christina admitted. "I just know that the last clue said time was running out. I don't like to think of Priscilla's life being in danger while we sit here running out of time to do anything about it."

Derian jumped up. "Then let's do something about it. I have an idea. Follow me!" Without waiting for an answer, he jumped up and skated back out of the cemetery and down the Freedom Trail toward the water at the bottom of the hill. The others followed him as fast as they could.

At the bottom of the hill, they were surprised to see

Freedom Trail

Copp's Hill Burying Ground

Derian stop a large yellow vehicle of some sort and talk to the driver who was sitting way up high. Behind the driver, also way up high in the open top vehicle, were a handful of weary-looking tourists.

"What's he up to?" Christina asked, as she caught up with the boys at the bottom of the hill. Before anyone could answer, Derian beckoned to them by waving his arm madly and screaming, "Come on! Hurry!"

As quickly as they could, the other kids got in line behind Derian and then climbed up into the vehicle and began to take seats.

"I talked him into letting us ride," Derian told them as they settled down. "By the way, you owe us ten bucks, princess. He's almost at the end of his route, and I told him we only need to get across–"

"Across what?" Christina demanded, just as Grant started squealing at the top of his lungs.

"What's wrong?" she asked him.

"We're going to drown!" he said. "This thing is going INTO THE WATER!" Sure enough, the vehicle had clambered down something that looked like a boat ramp and was now edging into the water. "Help!" Grant squealed.

Everyone on the boat began to laugh, but Grant

Copp's Hill
Burying Ground

USS
Constitution

looked like he was really, really upset.

"Hey, Grant," said C.F. "It's okay. This thing is called a Duck."

"No it's not!" said Grant, holding onto the side rail tightly as the vehicle went completely in the water and began to move away from the ramp. The distance between them and the shore increased rapidly, but Grant could tell that the crazy Duck-thing was indeed floating, even moving along rather quickly, as if it were a boat.

"Yes, Grant," Christina assured her brother. "It's a car and a boat. It's amphibious."

Now Grant really look puzzled, until his sister explained. "It's an amphibious vehicle; it's meant to travel on land and water. They used these things back in World War II. Now tourists ride them for fun . . . and in our case–convenience!"

Skeptically, Grant looked around at the other people on board and decided that they did look like they were enjoying themselves. He relaxed his grip on the railing. "Well you could have told me before we got on board," he grumbled.

"Sorry, squirt," said Derian. "I thought you knew what a Duck was."

Copp's Hill
Burying Ground

USS
Constitution

"I DO know what a duck is!" insisted Grant.

As the Duck headed toward the far shore, everyone grew quiet. The view of the famous Revolutionary War battle site, Bunker Hill, was beautiful in the dusk. The tall, granite obelisk monument glistened in the sunlight. It was here, in 1775, that the bloodiest battle of that war was fought, but the result had led to the eventual signing of the Declaration of Independence.

Soon, the *USS Constitution* came into view. The American flag at her stern fluttered proudly in the breeze. The enormous ship bobbed ever so slightly at its dock at Pier One.

"Wow," Grant whispered in awe. "That thing is huge!" He thought about how many afterschool hours it would have taken to paint that monster. Of course it might have been fun to help with back then, too. Maybe he would ask Papa if he could help paint *My Girl* next summer. Red, he thought–just like Mimi would want.

"Yeah, well it might not be here today if a bunch of school kids hadn't rescued it," C.F. said.

"What do you mean?" inquired Christina. "I don't remember reading about that last night."

Copp's Hill
Burying Ground

USS
Constitution

"Kids across the nation donated whatever money they could find to save the ship in the 1920s," Derian explained. "They held a 'penny drive' to collect millions of pennies and nickels to restore her back to the glory we see today."

Silently the kids observed the tall masts, ancient cannons, and yards of endless rigging.

Suddenly, there was a gentle bump as the Duck hit the ramp at the edge of the water.

"That's our cue!" C.F. hollered, startling all the other relaxed tourists. "Let's hit the road!"

The kids scurried in front of the tourists and bounded out of the boat. Grant, lugging his scooter along with him, landed on the ramp at the edge of the water. The scooter began to slide backwards, taking him into the water with a splash.

Holding onto the scooter for dear life, Grant began wading back ashore. "Hey, look!" he cried. "I am phibious, too!"

The kids and adults all laughed as he scrambled ashore. "I think you're a duck," Christina said, as she helped her wet, dripping, grinning brother up the ramp.

"That, too," said Grant with a laugh.

USS
Constitution

Freedom
Trail

15 NOT TILL YOU SEE THE WHITES OF THEIR EYES!

The kids headed straight for the ship. "You know," Christina whispered to Derian as they skated side-by-side, "Priscilla could be held hostage down in the hold of that ship."

"You have a pretty big imagination," Derian said. "But don't you think that's a little farfetched?"

"I'm just going by the clues," said Christina. "The kidnapper is trying to tell us something. But I can't figure out if he's trying to help us find Priscilla or trying to lead us away from her."

Before Derian could respond, they reached the enormous ship that was still the oldest commissioned warship afloat in the world.

"Old Ironsides!" C.F. said fondly as he looked up at the big ship. The setting sun was turning her hull's white

USS
Constitution

Freedom
Trail

stripe as pink as the pieces of paper the clues had been written on.

"Who's that?" Grant asked.

"The ship," said C.F. "During the War of 1812, cannonballs bounced off the hard hull of this ship so easily that the sailors nicknamed her Old Ironsides."

"There's only one problem," Derian said as they neared the dock. "The ship is closed for the night. See?"

On deck, a lone sailor played a mournful tune as two other sailors lowered the American flag.

"We can't get aboard?" Christina asked fearfully.

"Not tonight," said Derian.

Now the kids were really stumped. As they skated and scooted back out into the parking area, they saw a couple of racers stumbling to their cars with their numbers flapping loosely on their chests.

"Looks like the race is over," said Christina.

"Aw, it's been over for most of them by now," said Derian. "But folks will still be crossing the finish line even after dark."

"So there is still time?" Christina asked.

"Time for what?" said C.F.

"I don't know," said Christina, "but we can't give up.

USS
Constitution

Freedom
Trail

Your parents and our grandparents must be worried by now. We were supposed to meet at five, remember? At least *we* know Priscilla disappeared. But *they* only know she hasn't shown up at the finish line yet."

Grant had disappeared out of sight up a steep hill— Bunker Hill. The others followed him. The first real battle of the War for Independence was fought on this spot. Here the American colonists battled the British for the chance to create a new nation based on freedom. It was the place where the soldiers had been ordered, "Don't fire until you see the whites of their eyes!"

Like the *USS Constitution*, this historic site had also closed for the day. When Grant got to the top of the hill, he looked up at the obelisk and then down at the bulletin board which was empty except for opening and closing hours . . . and a pink note.

For some reason, the others stood aside as Christina approached the board and removed the note. In the growing dusk, she had to peer mightily at the faint pencil scribble to read the clue:

freedom
Trail

Bunker
Hill

For a moment the kids were silent. Then, Derian spoke. "So you mean this has all been a wild goose chase?"

"It sure sounds like it," said C.F.

Grant just frowned.

Christina could not talk at first; she felt like she might cry. Then she had an idea.

"How unCOMMONly stupid of him!" she said suddenly and started running for dear life.

16 BOSTON COMMON

With no idea of where she was headed or where they were going, the other kids dashed after Christina. They shouted at her to stop, which she only did when she finally got back to the pier where the Duck had docked.

"Oh, no," said Grant. "I'm not going Ducking again!"

"Fold up your scooter," Christina ordered him. "We don't have time for a Duck." Thrusting her arm up into the air, she hailed a taxicab parked across the street. The driver did a quick U-turn and stopped in front of the children.

"Where you wanna go, young lady?" the cabbie asked.

"Boston Common," Christina said urgently in her Southern drawl and plunged headfirst into the front seat of the taxi.

"Where?" the bewildered man repeated, looking at

Bunker
Hill

Boston
Common

107

Derian this time.

"BAH STAN KAH MAHN!" Derian said, as he yanked Grant into the backseat with him. The driver nodded and took off, barely giving C.F. time to slam the door behind him.

"What gives?" Derian asked Christina, tapping her shoulder hard over the seat. "You got money?"

The cabbie looked at her hard. "I've got money if it's not too far," Christina said.

"Not *where*?" the cabbie asked Derian.

"FAH, NOT FAR," Derian translated.

Christina didn't know how much to say in front of the taxi driver, but she could only see a few racers and other people left in the dusk on the road, so she just blurted out her thoughts.

"See, I think all these clues were scattered along the trail just to keep us occupied and as far from Priscilla as possible," she explained. "And I think the kidnapper had time to do this because he has Priscilla stashed somewhere where she can't get away."

"But why spend so much effort to keep a bunch of kids away?" C.F. asked.

Bunker
Hill

Boston
Common

"Because we are determined," Christina said. "There's four of us, and one of him. And we just kept going and going."

"Like the energizer duck," said Grant.

"Bunny!" they all yelled at him. "Energizer bunny."

"That doesn't matter," said Christina in aggravation. It was all but dark now, and the cabbie was zigzagging rapidly through the streets of Boston, coming close to the Common, Christina hoped. "What matters is that we get there in time. All day, the kidnapper has stayed with us to leave clues just in time for us to find them. I guess he figured we'd give up at dark. Then he made a mistake and left us that last insulting clue."

"What do you mean?" Derian asked.

"You know," said Christina. "the last clue that criticized us for not figuring out the end to all his stupid clues. But he made his mistake when he said COMMON instead of COME in the clue. He mistakenly said, 'How common you kids couldn't figure all this out.' He should have said, 'How come.' Personally, I think he made a Freudian slip."

"I thought it was a pink slip," said Grant.

"I mean he made a psychological slip-up," explained Christina.

"AH!" said Derian, catching on. "He should have said

Bunker
Hill

Boston
Common

'come,' but instead he said 'common'—so he gave something away by accident."

"Well," said Christina. "By accident or on purpose, I don't know which. But I think he was just ahead of us when he wrote that clue. After all, we were on skates by then."

"And Duck," added Grant.

"And Duck," Christina agreed. "The last clue was scribbled so fast that I could hardly read it, so I guess he was in a hurry to mislead us one last time and then head back to Priscilla."

"Probably to spirit her out of town now that the race traffic has died down," Derian said.

"Or worse," said Christina.

The taxi swerved left and right, then screeched to a halt. Christina began to dig all the money she had left out of all her pockets and piled it into the driver's hand.

"But where is Priscilla?" C.F. asked.

Christina waved her free hand all around. "Right here, I hope," she said. "Right here in Boston Common!"

"BAH STAN KAH MAHN!" the driver called after them as the kids dashed into the park.

Bunker
Hill

Boston
Common

17 MAKE WAY FOR THE KIDS

The park was dark. It was a great place to play in the daylight. Lots of green grass and beautiful trees. Beautiful blue lakes with little bridges over them. Plenty of flowers. And best of all were the Swan Boats you could ride in the summer months. Christina remembered coming to Boston with Grandmother Mimi once before when she was as young as Grant. The thing she remembered as the most special was Mimi reading *Make Way for Ducklings,* and then taking her for a ride on a Swan Boat in the pretty blue Lagoon of the Public Garden.

The lights in the park were dim and the many curving pathways went from one dark place to another. In one corner of the park, they spotted two runners kissing. On another corner, a policewoman on

Boston Common

Boston Public Gardens

horseback chatted with another runner. So without being noticed, the kids crept down the park paths, deeper into the Common.

"This place is uncommonly creepy," Grant said.

"All these dark shadows sure give *me* the creeps," said C.F.

"There sure are plenty of places to hide . . . or hide a body," Derian added.

Grant moaned. "Please don't say *body*."

Christina rubbed her brother's tired, sloping little shoulders. "Don't worry," she said.

"Sorry about that," said Derian "Think positive. Think about summer. Think about cooling off under the fountain in the Frog Pond, riding the Swan Boats in the Garden, or having a picnic under the willows."

Now they were in what seemed to be the darkest part of the park. All these charming details didn't sound so interesting right now, even if they painted a pretty picture.

Pretty picture. Christina wondered–could it be? Why did she have the feeling that the only good place to hide someone in this park was in the last place anyone would suspect. After all, they wouldn't even begin to use them until . . .

Boston
Common

Boston
Public
Gardens

Suddenly Derian blurted out, "Well, I think that we're working on getting lost. C.F. and I are a long way from knowing this park like the backs of our hands, especially in the dark. This park is huge, so there are plenty of places for us to get lost."

"I don't *do* lost," Grant insisted.

"One lost person at a time is plenty," C.F. agreed.

But Christina just charged full steam ahead down the path. She called back over her shoulder. "But I'm not lost! I know exactly where I'm going, and that's exactly where Priscilla is!"

18 WELL, I SWAN!

As they rounded a dark path, they came up to the main lake in the park. Beside the lake was a shed where the Swan Boats were stored. Bravely, Christina went right up to the stack of boats. They were dirty and cobwebby from being stored there all winter. The others followed her then stopped cold as they heard her begin to call, "Priscilla? Priscilla?"

Just as the others were about to question Christina's sanity, a weak voice responded from beneath one of the overturned boats. "Yes! It's me!! Help me!!! Please!!!!"

"We're coming!" Derian cried and ran to untangle the chain that not only held the boat to the ground but was wrapped around his sister's waist, wrists, and ankles, keeping her trapped. As he pulled the boat upward, the other kids helped free the shivering woman. Gently,

Boston
Public Gardens

The Swan
Boats

Christina pulled the duct tape that had covered Priscilla's mouth.

"I just got that duct tape loosened enough in time to answer you," Priscilla said. "I've been trapped here all day. How in the world did you find me?"

But before Christina could answer her relieved cousin, a man came up behind them and said, "With my *clues!*"

They all whirled around to see a young, scraggly-bearded man pointing a gun at them. "Nobody's rescued— in fact, you're all caught!"

As he moved toward them, they all inched back toward the Swan Boats. The man picked up the end of the heavy chain. "Plenty of time to chain you all together and launch you in one of these leaky, old boats," he said with a nasty grin. "Should only take minutes for it to sink in the deepest part of the lake. It'll be hard to swim with this heavy chain wrapped around you," he said, and let out a horrid laugh.

Christina knew what Papa would say to do if you found a person pointing a gun at you. Be still! So she did, and hoped that the boys would not try to pull any rescue hero theatrics and put them all in any more deadly danger. And they all did freeze perfectly still. All except for Grant.

Suddenly, Grant whipped the tiny flashlight Uncle

The Swan
Boats

Uh Oh!

Christina in the Boston Common

Michael had given him out of his pocket. He flicked it on and shone it directly into the man's eyes. "Make way for the Duckling Sleuths!" he cried. As if on cue, all the kids yelled and darted toward the blinded man's legs, tackling him to the ground.

He still had the gun in his hand and was bringing it down to aim at them when a bright flashlight burst on. A gloved hand grabbed the gun and quickly snatched it away.

The kids looked up from their heap on the ground. It was the mounted policewoman and the cabbie.

"I knew when these crazy kids wanted to come to the Bahstan Kahman at night and were talking about kidnapping and stuff, that something bad was up," the cabbie said.

"You did the right thing to tell me," the officer assured him. "Now everybody stand up and start explaining yourselves!"

The Swan Boats

Uh Oh!

19 No Time to Waste!

The children stood up on shaking knees. The policewoman handcuffed the man and yanked him to his feet. The cabbie helped Priscilla out from under the boat and put his jacket around her shivering shoulders.

"All right, who's going first?" the officer demanded.

"I-I-I will," said Priscilla, her voice sounding more angry than scared. "I know this guy." She pointed at the bearded man. "He is the parent of one of my students. I had to fail the boy. His Dad warned me he would hurt me if I did that, but I never believed him. I had to put the good of my student first and he really needed to repeat a grade. I promised to tutor him for free, but even that didn't satisfy his father."

"What do you know about kids!" the man blurted out, pulling at the handcuffs and the officer's hold.

Uh Oh!

An Arrest!

121

"She's a teacher!" Christina cried. "She loves kids!"

Suddenly, she and Priscilla were holding one another and crying.

Now Derian was angry. "She was running in the Boston Marathon to show kids that you can achieve anything you try," he said. "Even if you have to try over and over. Even if you don't finish first. Even if . . ."

Before Derian could finish, they all looked at Grant's big eyes. He looked like he had seen a ghost behind them. Slowly they all turned, even the policewoman's horse, to see where Grant was staring.

"Oh boy," he said, "Now we are all in BIG trouble!"

It was Papa. And Mimi. And Aunt Emma and Uncle Fritz. Papa looked very angry. He stalked right up to the kids, ignoring the officer and everyone else, as if it were common to find an arrest going on in the dark in the park.

He grabbed the four kids and hugged them tightly. "Where have you characters been? You have worried us to death!"

Aunt Emma and Uncle Fritz grabbed Priscilla and hugged her. Mimi, however, stood there looking at the bad guy with a face so fierce it was scarier than a pirate's scowl.

Uh Oh!

An Arrest!

"We'll get to the bottom of this later down at the police station," she told the officer, as if she were in charge. "But right now . . ."

Mimi turned and went to Priscilla. "You okay?"

Priscilla gave her a weak smile. "I am now," she said.

"Then let's go!" said Mimi. "There's no time to waste!"

Uh Oh!

An Arrest!

20 THE FINISH LINE

Before anyone knew what was going on, everyone was piled into Uncle Fritz's SUV and speeding down the street. The kids had no idea what was going on, but as soon as Priscilla figured it out, she began to laugh and cry at the same time.

"You can't really mean . . ." she began.

"We sure can!" the other adults shouted back at her.

In an instant, Uncle Fritz stopped the SUV. Papa helped Priscilla out onto the dark race course. Mimi and Aunt Emma herded the kids down the road a bit to a certain spot to face her.

"Runner, take your mark!" Papa shouted.

Uncle Fritz slammed his hands together in a "gunshot" crack!

Still laughing and crying, Priscilla began to run. She

Boston
Common

The Finish
Line!

stumbled and bobbled at first, then in the cool night air, she threw her shoulders back and picked up speed.

Off the side of the road, Papa turned on Uncle Fritz's big spotlight and aimed it at a sign over the road. Other people had begun to gather around to see what was going on. They began to clap their hands, whistle, and cheer Priscilla on!

As she crossed the finish line, Mimi, Aunt Emma, and all the kids hugged her as tightly as they could. Everyone was cheering and crying and laughing now.

"I really was determined to finish this race—my first Boston Marathon," Priscilla said, catching a sob in her throat.

"We know you were," said her mother, giving her another hug.

"But I must say my time must be the worst of anyone's," Priscilla added with a sniffle.

"I think your family and students will be as proud of you as if you had common first place!" Papa said with a roar.

The kids began laughing.

"Papa," Christina said, "You said common instead of come."

"I guess that was a Freudian slip," said Grant.

Boston
Common

The finish
Line!

"But I don't wear a slip!" said Papa, and the kids laughed even harder.

After a lot of handshakes all around and some picture-making (with flash!), they piled back into the SUV and headed to the police station for their other unfinished business.

It took about an hour for Priscilla to explain that the man who had kidnapped her was mentally disturbed. He was upset about possibly losing custody of his child and had taken his anguish out on her. She really wanted him to get treatment instead of going to jail, but the officer said that holding a gun on a Boston Marathon runner and a bunch of kids was pretty serious business, so the judge would have to decide.

It took another hour for Christina and the rest of the kids to explain about the pink clues, the wild goose chase down the Freedom Trail, and Christina's hunch about the Boston Common and the Swan Boats. The kids got tired of explaining, and the adults got tired of not understanding and so the whole matter finally got dropped except for why they were now the apparent owners of some beat-up old rollerblades and a bent

Boston
Common

The Finish
Line!

scooter.

"Uh, yeah. These probably need to go back to the church at some point," C.F. said sheepishly with a sideways glance at the pile of discarded contraband.

The taxi driver tried to do some explaining, but his BAHSTAN accent was so thick that no one could understand him except Uncle Fritz, who just patted him on the back and said, "AH KNOW JUST WHAT YAH MEAN!"

When everyone was done explaining, Priscilla expressed everyone's sentiment by proclaiming, "I am uncommonly hungry!"

"Well, I can sure fix that," said Uncle Fritz, pulling out his keys.

"Legal Sea Foods?" the kids all squealed together hopefully.

"I could even eat illegal seafood," said Grant.

"I could eat a giant lobster!" said Derian.

"I could eat a lot of big, fat shrimp!" said C.F.

"I could eat a fathom of fish!" said Christina.

Grant rubbed his tummy in a big, round circle. "Well, I could eat a Duck!" he said.

Everyone got quiet.

"A duck?" said Papa.

We found Priscilla!

"Sure," said Grant. "Duck seems to be good for just about anything: Duck boats. Duck tape. Duck . . ."

Grant's list was drowned out by the sound of laughter. Papa slung Grant up onto his shoulders and led the way out of the police station. When they got to the doorway, Papa cried up to Grant, "Be sure and DUCK!"

The Finish!

The Finish Line

Legal Sea Foods

ABOUT THE AUTHOR

Carole Marsh is an author and publisher who has written many works of fiction and non-fiction for young readers. She travels throughout the United States and around the world to research her books. In 1979 Carole Marsh was named Communicator of the Year for her corporate communications work with major national and international corporations.

Marsh is the founder and CEO of Gallopade International, established in 1979. Today, Gallopade International is widely recognized as a leading source of educational materials for every state and many countries. Marsh and Gallopade were recipients of the 2002 Teachers' Choice Award. Marsh has written more than 13 Carole Marsh Mysteries™. Years ago, her children, Michele and Michael, were the original characters in her mystery books. Today, they continue the Carole Marsh Books tradition by working at Gallopade. By adding grandchildren Grant and Christina as new mystery characters, she has continued the tradition for a third generation.

Ms. Marsh welcomes correspondence from her readers. You can e-mail her at carole@gallopade.com, visit the carolemarshmysteries.com website, or write to her in care of Gallopade International, P.O. Box 2779, Peachtree City, Georgia, 30269 USA.

Gallopade International is proud to be a member of the National School Supply and Equipment Association, the National Social Studies Council, the Association for Supervision and Curriculum Development, the Museum Store Association, and the Association of Partners for Public Lands.

GLOSSARY

amphibious: operating on land and water

columns: tall pillars used in architecture

contraband: illegal, prohibited, or smuggled goods

dingy: dirty and shabby conditions

duel: a formal battle between two people to solve an argument by drawing guns or swords on each other

eccentric: someone who does things strangely or oddly

exasperate: to frustrate or annoy

famished: being really, really, really hungry!

freighters: big ocean-going ships that carry lots of cargo

harbor: bay or gulf where many ships come in and out

hectare: a metric measurement like an acre

hull: the tough outer shell of a ship

illegal: against the law

marathon: a long race; a challenge

mast: tall pole that goes down through the deck and into the hull of a ship that supports the sails

monument: a memorial stone, structure, sculpture or building designed to remember a person or event

nemesis: an enemy

obelisk: a four-sided pillar that gradually tapers as it rises upward into a pyramid shape

passel: a big number or quantity of something; a whole lot

red herring: a false clue

rigging: network of ropes and ladders that sailors use to raise, move and control a ship's sails

sashay: to walk about with a bold and flippant manner

sexton: religious leader that helps run the church

skeptically: with doubt or hesitation

stern: the rear end of a ship or boat

swatch: a small piece of fabric

taxation: extra government fees, to be collected and used for public services and/or improvements

theatrics: dramatic and silly actions

vestibule: the lobby before a main room

Boston Marathon

Recipe for fun: Read the book, take the tour, find the items on this list and check them off! (Hint: Look high and low!!) *Teachers: you have permission to reproduce this form for your students.*

__1. Beacon Hill

__2. Boston Common

__3. Brattle Book Shop

__4. Bunker Hill Monument

__5. clock hands

__6. cobblestones

__7. Duck

__8. gold dome

__9. historic marker

__10. a lobster

SCAVENGER HUNT!

__11. Old North Church

__12. Old State House

__13. Park Street Church

__14. patriot statue

__15. Quincy Market

__16. Swan Boats

__17. steeple

__18. The "T"

__19. tombstones

__20. *USS Constitution*

Enjoy this exciting excerpt from

THE MYSTERY OF BILTMORE HOUSE

1 FOUR HOT, SWEATY, CRAZY, MAD KIDS

Stacy Brown dealt the cards into the sloppy stacks in the back seat of the red station wagon. She snapped each card with as loud a pop as she could. She was mad.

"That sure doesn't sound like homework," her mom commented from the front seat.

Snap. "School's". . . *pop* . . ."out," Stacy reminded her.

Her mom mumbled and Stacy mumbled back. School was out, and all of her friends were starting their part-time summer jobs. All except her. And here she was stuck in Asheville on her way to the Biltmore House where she had been a hundred . . . thousand . . . million times before. Just because her mom had to help coordinate a mystery writing workshop being held at the estate this week.

Stacy had a part-time job at a kennel all lined up. She needed money badly. There was an international dog show in California, where she used to live, the next week. And, boy, did she want to go. Shoot, she'd been showing dogs since she was a puppy herself. She'd won lots of prizes. But this worldwide meet would be just wonderful. The time was right. It was for kids just her age, thirteen. And her dog was in perfect condition.

Her mom always said you have to make things happen. So Stacy had worked hard to get that job to make enough money to go. But now her mom was making her tag along with her like she was a baby or something.

Next to showing dogs, Stacy's favorite thing was playing bridge. But it didn't seem like much fun today in the hot, sweaty back seat playing all four hands by herself.

Stacy saw her mom look at her in the rearview mirror. Spy, Stacy thought. I'm being watched. She could see her mom frown at her windblown hair and her skirt that was wrinkled from sprawling in a not too ladylike position, trying to make room for invisible bridge partners. Stacy turned her face where her mom couldn't see it and made an awful face.

Why did they have to meet the others here at historic Biltmore Village? Why couldn't they have met them at the McDonald's across the street where they had civilization — milk shakes?

The blue Mustang sped down I-26 toward the mountains. He's gonna get a ticket, the boy in the back seat thought. He stared up into the sky looking for a blue light to come from outer space and pull them over. Nothing. Shucks.

Trent Evans swiped a thin streak of perspiration above his lip. "Air," he moaned dramatically from the back seat. "Air!"

He pretended he was being kidnapped and held hostage. Didn't that happen recently somewhere between Spartanburg and Asheville? Any minute he was going to be tossed in the trunk where summer had been stored since last year. Maybe his dad could put that in a mystery story.

Somehow, while all his friends were heading the opposite direction, toward the cool South Carolina coast, he was trapped into going with his dad to a writing workshop in Asheville.

He didn't even know his dad wanted to be a writer. He wasn't a writer. He was an engineer. But the textile plant he worked for had some temporary layoffs. His dad was always telling him when life gives you lemons, make lemonade. And so he had decided that instead of moping around the house worrying about lost hours, he would try his hand at writing.

Trent was sure it had all been his mother's idea. He knew that it had been her idea that this would be a great time for father and son to get to know each other better.

Trent sank back into the hot cushion and watched the mountains get larger before his very eyes. "I'll bet I could get to know Dad real good at the beach," he muttered. "Besides, if you don't know your dad by the time you're eleven, when are you supposed to know him?"

Wendy and Michael Hunt sat glumly in the back seat of the car. They were both hunched over some of Mother's long pads of yellow paper. Michael was inventing a new video game where a horrid monster gobbled up big sisters. Wendy was writing notes about which cute fourth grade girl Michael was in love with to pay him back.

Suddenly, the car swerved left, then right, tossing their papers out of their hands. Mother never takes the straight route, Wendy thought. We could have gotten on the interstate and made it from Tryon to Asheville in thirty minutes. But if there was a long way around, Mother always took it.

Mother's camera equipment and trusty rusty typewriter were piled up on the seat beside her. She never went anywhere without either one. "A tornado might come charging down the road and I wouldn't want to miss it," she would always say. I can just picture her making a picture of us getting scooped up by some big black inverted triangle, Wendy thought.

Michael was mad, too. It had been his turn to ride in the front. But they had argued about it and so Mother had pointed them both to the back seat. It was going to be a long, hot summer, he decided. And what a way to start – going to a big, old house so his mother could attend a writing workshop. She'd written a bunch of books – why did she need more courses, he wondered. Then he remembered. She wasn't taking a class, she was teaching one. As if being a mother weren't bad enough, now she was going to be a teacher, too. The thought of the combination gave him cold chills up his hot backbone.

At precisely the same time, two cars whipped into the steaming asphalt parking places beside Stacy's car. A white car on the left; a blue one on the right. She felt like she was in the middle of a twelve-wheeled American flag. A fast glimpse showed her there was one boy in one car and a boy and girl in the other. A foursome for bridge, she thought. Then she frowned. They probably didn't like cards. They probably won't like me. And I'll bet they don't want to be here any more than I do.

The adults all hopped out of the cars and met on the sidewalk. Stacy could tell from the nodding and shaking of hands that introductions were being made all around. The kids just sat in the cars and stared meanly at one another, as though it was the others' fault they were here.

The adults chuckled. As her mom got back in the car, Stacy heard her say loudly enough for the kids to hear, "I have the perfect thing to cheer this hot bunch up before we head for Biltmore House."

Stacy scooped all her cards into a pile and stacked them up in record time. As if she was jumping hurdles, she bounded over the seats into the front one beside her mom. She knew what that meant.

Trent stared at the crazy girl in the car next to him. He was puzzled by her hopping around. Then she was even more puzzled when she waved gaily at him.

Wendy and Michael looked through the steamy window at the strange girl in the next car. She turned and smiled at them. "Whatever she's got to be happy about is a mystery to me," Wendy muttered.

Spreading the tips of his fingers up to the edge of the window, Michael waved and smiled back at the mysterious-acting girl.

Enjoy this exciting excerpt from

THE MYSTERY OF BLACKBEARD THE PIRATE

1 A STOLEN HEAD

"His head is missing?" Mother asked with a laugh.

Michele, who was pecking out her name - Michele Hunt, age twelve - on the typewriter in the breakfast room, paused to listen to her mother's strange phone call.

"Oh, I'm sorry," her mother said, now with a serious tone in her voice. "I didn't realize the loss of the head could mean such a terrible tragedy."

Michele listened intently now. What in the world could Mother be talking about, she wondered.

Her brother, Michael, sneaked into the living room through the side door. Michele guessed he didn't want Mother to see that he was soaked with soap and water from washing the car. He was a little short to be seven and had to climb all over the sudsy car to reach the top.

Tiptoeing into the breakfast room, he mouthed a "Where's Mom?"

Yuck, Michele grimaced, even his mouth was foamy. She whispered "Shhh," and pointed to the yellow paper hanging in the typewriter. She began to type slowly in the rhythmic pace Mother said would help increase her speed. She had started typing lessons as soon as school was out so she would be ready for the drama club she wanted so badly to be in next year. She thought that if she were able to type scripts, it might help her get accepted.

She had seen a Broadway show when she went with her Mother to New York City to see a publisher. Ever since, she'd been hooked on the theatre. It just seemed to offer something for everyone, no matter what your talents.

Michael leaned over Michele's shoulder and watched as she typed:

"His head is missing . . ."

He squiggled his nose and squinted his eyes like he always did when he didn't understand something but didn't want to admit it.

Mother came around the corner to the breakfast room. She stretched the phone cord and sat down on the bench across the table from them, still listening carefully to the caller.

She smiled at Michael and Michele and gave them that loving once-over Michele knew so well. She would always start at their pale blonde hair, then look them both deep in their blue eyes and round faces, like she was looking into a mirror back in time, perhaps when she was their age.

The three of them looked so much alike it was incredible. People would always comment about it when they went anywhere together. Even their bald-headed baby pictures all looked alike. The comments always made Michele feel a little self-conscious, and Michael always scrooched up his face.

Mother shook her head slowly. "Now I'm not really sure I want the kids to come down," she said to the caller. "It may not be safe."

She handed the receiver to Michael to hang back up, then stared blankly out the window. "Bath," she said absent-mindedly.

"Mom," moaned Michael, slapping his arms against his sides with a squish-splat. "I can't get much cleaner than this."

Mother looked at him and laughed. "If the car's as clean as you are, you've earned your three bucks," she said. "But I don't mean tub bath. I mean Bath — Bath, North Carolina."

Sometimes Mother didn't seem to make a lot of sense, but it was one of the things Michele loved best about her. They both loved words. But her Mother, who ran a small advertising agency and could write a perfect sentence, always talked in twists and turns.

"Do you mean *Bath* is a place?" asked Michele.

"I do — and you and Michael are going to spend about six

weeks there this summer with John. I have an out of town assignment that will take me that long, but I'll be down on weekends."

"Oh, Mother," Michele and Michael groaned together. "No!"

"We want to spend the summer with our friends at the pool," Michele said.

"Yeah, and we have tickets to the summer movies," added Michael.

"Please don't do this to us," Michele begged. "We'll just die."

"You'll live," she assured them. "Bath's a pretty coastal town on the Pamlico Sound. John is staying in a nice motel on Bath Creek. He's doing some historical research, so he can give you a real basement-to-attic tour of the historic homes there."

"Ugh," pouted Michael. "Is there a pool?" he asked, sliding off of the bench and onto the floor.

Mother shook her head. "Nope, no pool."

"A movie or skating rink?" Michele questioned, afraid she already knew the answer.

Mother's hair swished negatively again. "No, sorry," she said.

"Phooey," Michael mumbled from under the table.

Michele knew he was really upset. She was too, but hated to show it. Her Mother had to travel a good bit for her job and Michele knew it was difficult for her to get care for them since her Mother and Father were divorced. Mom was very particular about who she left them with and Michele figured she must have gone to a lot of trouble to arrange for them to stay with John in Bath.

John was nice, but she sure wanted to stay home this summer. Why did it seem like things always turned out differently than you planned them? It was just like her typing. She would aim for an *a* but strike the *z*.

"Well, Bath does have one redeeming factor, if you want to call it that," Mother said mysteriously. "Blackbeard lived there."

Michael popped up from under the table and screwed his nose and eyes together in disbelief.

"*The* Blackbeard?" he asked.

"No Michael, the other Blackbeard," Michele teased.

"Blackbeard, the fiercest pirate of them all," Mother said.

Michele sighed, revealing the dismay she'd been trying to conceal. "Well, I guess we could spend the summer looking for treasure."

"Be sure and check Teach's Hole," Mother advised.

"I wish they would put *my* teacher in a hole," said Michael.

"*Teach's* Hole," repeated Mother. "That's where Blackbeard fought his last skull-and-crossbones battle. He lost it," she said in a deep, lateshow-spook-movie voice. "And he lost his head."

"Is *that* the head you said was missing?" cried Michele. She blushed, realizing she'd just given away that she'd been eavesdropping.

"Big ears!" Mother said. "I guess you could say that

Blackbeard the Pirate's head is missing — missing from his body. But the head they're searching so frantically for in Bath belongs to the living Blackbeard."

She sighed and said seriously, as though again reconsidering letting them go to Bath. "They must find it soon. It may be life or death for the play."

"What living Blackbeard? What head? What play?" Michele begged.

"They have an outdoor drama in Bath every summer," Mother explained. "The play is about Blackbeard and pirates and Bath. They stage it in an outdoor theatre by the water."

"You mean you just sit right outside with no roof?" asked Michael.

"The sky is your roof," Michele said, then added quickly, "But what about the head?"

"In the play, just as happened in real life, Blackbeard is killed at Teach's Hole off Ocracoke Island. They chop off his head," Mother said. "At the climax of the drama they have a big pirate battle and end the play by holding up Blackbeard's gruesome-looking head. It's supposed to be very realistic and dramatic. But now the head is missing."

"Why don't they just make another one?" Michele asked.

"That takes time and money," Mother said. "The play is very expensive to produce and they don't try to make any money — just cover expenses. Opening night is in a couple of weeks. They need to recover the head, and find out who would risk the play's success like that — and why."

To Michele, summer in Bath was beginning to sound more

mysterious, and therefore, more fun every minute.

"Tell us more about Bath," Michele said.

"Bath is North Carolina's oldest town, incorporated in 1705," Mother explained. "They have restored several historic homes. The play and the homes bring needed income to the community. A lot of mysterious shenanigans won't help the tourist business any. And, no tourists — no play!"

Suddenly, Michael grabbed his neck as though he were trying to pluck it from his shoulders. "Yiiii, ye got me head," he moaned.

Mother laughed. "If somebody chopped off your head today, they'd get squirted with soapsuds instead of blood," she said, taking the kitchen towel and rubbing his hair.

"Yiiii, it was me own Mother," Michael squealed, holding his neck and letting his head flop left and right under the towel.

"But who would steal the head and jeopardize the play?" pondered Michele.

Mother laughed. "A play's the ultimate treasure, hey? I don't know who would steal a costume head," she said, looking worried. "But John promised he would keep you two, as well as Jo Dee and Brian, from playing detective until it's found and the play can begin."

"Who's Jo Dee?" Michael asked excitedly. He poked his head out from under the towel. "Who's Brian? Does he have a head?"

"John's two children will be staying with him this summer," Mother explained.

"Oh brother," groaned Michele. "I guess I'll have to

babysit." That's what summer had meant for the last couple of years since Mother started working. Michele had to watch Michael several mornings or afternoons each week, and she liked for them to stay close to home. Of course it meant extra spending money, and Michele had to admit it was hard to find ways to earn money when you're only twelve.

"Brian's thirteen, so I doubt he'd appreciate you as a babysitter," Mother said.

"Super!" said Michael. "Is Jo Dee a boy too?"

"Sorry, Jo Dee is a ten-year-old girl," Mother said.

"Girls! They're taking over the world!" Michael complained. "They're everywhere, and they're all older than me. It isn't fair!"

Michele laughed. She guessed it was hard sometimes to be the youngest and the only boy in the family, especially now with Dad not around. She knew Michael missed him. Maybe that's why Mom had arranged for them to stay with John for awhile, she thought.

Mother swatted Michael's hair with the towel once more and stood up. "I'd better fix you pirates some grog and hardtack for lunch," she said and went into the kitchen.

"We'll find the head when we're in Bath," Michele whispered to Michael, hoping Mother wasn't eavesdropping.

"Phooey with Blackbeard's head," said Michael, "let's find his treasure!" He watched as Michele pecked out on the typewriter:

"Who has the head? Why? What will they do next?"